Close encounters of the most terrifying kind

I scream; I can't help it. Tim screams too. And when we stop screaming we hear the high-pitched, soft chittering sounds coming from the backseat. And something laps my neck again.

I'm not thinking, and Tim isn't either, because at the same instant we both bolt from the car, Tim clutching his portfolio. But then, for some reason, we can't run. There are dark shapes all around us, graceful, undulating, like they're moving underwater. Not human shapes. They're touching me damply, pulling at my clothes. I scream again; I've never been so terrified in my life. And yet I just can't run away; it's like some kind of force is stopping me. All I can do is let them guide me—their voices whistling breathily—toward the amber lights, on the ground now, very close to the car. . . .

PUFFIN BOOKS BY WILLIAM SLEATOR

WILLIAM SLEATOR

THE NIGHT THE HEADS CAME

PUFFIN BOOKS

PUFFIN BOOKS
Published by the Penguin Group
Penguin Putnam Inc., 375 Hudson Street, New York, New York 10014, U.S.A.
Penguin Books Ltd, 27 Wrights Lane, London W8 5TZ, England
Penguin Books Australia Ltd, Ringwood, Victoria, Australia
Penguin Books Canada Ltd, 10 Alcorn Avenue, Toronto, Ontario, Canada M4V 3B2
Penguin Books (N.Z.) Ltd, 182-190 Wairau Road, Auckland 10, New Zealand

Penguin Books Ltd, Registered Offices: Harmondsworth, Middlesex, England

First published in the United States of America by Dutton Children's Books,
a division of Penguin Books USA Inc., 1996
Published in Puffin Books, 1998

10 9 8 7 6 5 4 3 2 1

THE LIBRARY OF CONGRESS HAS CATALOGED THE DUTTON EDITION AS FOLLOWS:
Sleator, William.
The night the heads came/William Sleator.
—1st ed. p. cm.
Summary: When aliens abduct both Leo and his artist friend Tim,
Leo tries to determine why these creatures from outer space
want particularly to use his friend's talent.
ISBN 0-525-45463-2 (hc)
[1. Extraterrestrial beings—Fiction. 2. Science fiction.]
I. Title. PZ7.S6313Ni 1996
[Fic]—dc20 95-32321 CIP AC

Puffin Books ISBN 0-14-038441-3

Printed in the United States of America

For my niece and nephew,

Julie and Spencer Wald,

who have not been

abducted—yet

CHAPTER ONE

"I STILL THINK YOU'RE CRAZY," I TELL TIM.

"Can you go any faster, Leo?" he says, looking at his watch. He's nervous about getting to Bridgetown by midnight, when the bus to New York stops there.

It's very dark outside the car. There are no lights, no houses or factories, no other cars on this isolated stretch of two-lane road.

"What if your parents saw you getting into my car?" I ask him, not for the first time. "You're not the one who's going to be around tomorrow when they figure out you took that money and didn't come back. You're not the one who's going to have to figure out what to say, like to the cops. You're not the one who's going to—"

"Just tell them you don't know anything," he says dismissively, shoving more potato chips into his mouth. Then he groans. "What am I going to do if the people in New York hate the rest of my drawings?"

I sigh, gripping the wheel in frustration, my eyes on the two headlight beams on the narrow road. Tim knows I have major difficulty lying to anybody about anything. But he's not worried about the problems he's leaving behind for me to deal with; all he's thinking about is his artwork. He has an appointment with a publisher, who expressed interest in the science fiction drawings Tim sent—nothing is more important to Tim than his drawings. I'm helping him get to New York because I understand why he wants to make this bid for independence from his parents; they've always been controlling, and recently they've gotten even worse than usual. I just wish he could wait another year, until we're out of high school, so there wouldn't be such a big mess about it.

I also kind of resent him for asking me to do this, since he knew I wouldn't be able to say no, being his best friend. So here I am, driving him to Bridgetown, getting implicated.

"Could you step on it a little?" he says, using his irritating, whiny voice. "It's eleven thirty-five. I've *got* to catch that bus!"

"I *am* stepping on it," I say. "But there's something funny about the accelerator. Like it's sluggish. It's weird. Dad just got the car tuned last week."

"I hope you're not running out of gas. You know there's nothing between here and Bridgetown."

"I filled it on the way over to your house, fatso."

"Oh, so now you're picking on me for being fat!"

"Oh, I am not! But do you really think I'd forget to—"

"Hey! Over there on the right. You see those lights?"

I look away from the road. I've never seen a circle of lights in the sky like that, a peculiar kind of amber color. I know there are no buildings around here, and those lights are too low to be an airplane. Anyway, airplanes don't just hang there. "You think it's a helicopter, maybe?"

"What would a helicopter be doing around here? Unless they've already got the cops after us." Tim turns abruptly back to me. "Hey, what's the matter? Why are you slowing down *now?*"

"I'm not slowing down. The car's acting crazy. Like it's—"

And then the lights go out and the engine dies and the whir of the air conditioner shuts off. I can't see a thing. I slam on the brakes, afraid the car's going to go off the road in the sudden blackness. The tires squeal; the car swerves; there's the crunch of gravel. Finally the car stops. At least we still seem to be on the road.

"What are you *doing?*" Tim shouts at me.

"I'm trying to start this thing. It just died, for no reason," I shout back at him, panicking, frantically turning the key in the ignition, pumping the accelerator. Nothing happens.

"Great!" Tim says. "Just wonderful. Your battery dies out here in the middle of nowhere. My career is over." He groans again, and I hear the sound of his fists pounding on the seat—it's too dark for me to even see

Tim. "Why didn't you go the other way? At least then I could have hitched," he accuses me.

"Oh, shut up! You know we had to go this way so no one would see us," I argue, still uselessly trying to start the car. It's completely silent out here. The only sound is the click of the key in the ignition.

Until we hear the scratching on the windows.

My whole body jerks. I let go of the key. "What was that? A bird or something?" I whisper.

"I can't see any more than you can," Tim whispers back, and I wonder if I sound as scared as he does.

The scratching continues, on my side as well as Tim's. Soft but sharp, like stones being gently scraped against the glass.

"Quick, lock your door! And the back one too," I say, still whispering. We have to do it manually, of course. I squirm around in the seat to press the lock on the door behind me.

But I can't find it. Because the door behind me is already open. I feel the warm air blowing in. And then a delicate touch on the back of my neck, rough and moist and cold, like an animal's tongue. A dead animal, from the smell of it.

I scream; I can't help it. Tim screams too. And when we stop screaming we hear the high-pitched, soft chittering sounds coming from the backseat. And something laps my neck again.

I'm not thinking, and Tim isn't either, because at

the same instant we both bolt from the car, Tim clutching his portfolio. But then, for some reason, we can't run. There are dark shapes all around us, graceful, undulating, like they're moving underwater. Not human shapes. They're touching me damply, pulling at my clothes. I scream again; I've never been so terrified in my life. And yet I just can't run away; it's like some kind of force is stopping me. All I can do is let them guide me—their voices whistling breathily—toward the amber lights, on the ground now, very close to the car.

Up a ramp, into a very dimly lit place. The rotten smell is stronger here. The shapes gently push me down; I'm sitting on something spongelike and slimy. What feels like a rubber cable instantly wraps itself around my waist and stays there. I pull at it; I try to squirm away, shouting again, but the cable is locked in place around me. Tim is shouting too.

And then I can't shout; I'm gulping, because the place we're in shoots suddenly into the air, like a silent supersonic elevator. My stomach drops away. I can't see outside, but I don't need to see to feel how incredibly swiftly we're zooming up, up, and up. I'm gasping now, panting, sweating. The creatures don't seem to mind the sensation; they're making those swimming movements around us. There's not enough light in here to see what they look like; they're still just dark shapes. I don't *want* to see what they look like; all I want is to be out of here.

And then, with a sudden jolt, we stop. The cable slides away from my waist. Directly ahead of me a light appears, growing, a round door opening like the aperture around the lens on a camera.

And now I can see the creatures. I flinch away from them and squeeze my eyes shut. They don't pay any attention. They're prodding me again, up off the seat, moving me forward, making me walk. And I can't resist it; I have to go where they're taking me; I have to walk—meaning I have to open my eyes.

The creatures are tall, taller than Tim and me, with two long, pale arms that seem boneless, like tentacles. I can tell they are very thin, even though they are wearing loose, sleeveless robes that hang from their long necks to the floor. The truly horrible thing about them is their heads, simply because they are so tiny in relation to their height, about the size of tennis balls. The heads are smooth and gray and almost featureless, with one lidless eye in the front and another in the back, and underneath the eyes a mouth like a line without lips that seems to go all the way around the head. In fact, looking at their heads and the way they move, it becomes apparent that these creatures don't *have* a front or a back; they are the same on both sides, gliding backward or forward without having to turn around.

They lead us through the round opening, out of the small ship that brought us here, down a corridor, into a very large space lit by an all-pervasive amber glow. I can't tell exactly how big the room is because it's full of foliage—foliage that gently rustles and sways, though there is no breeze. Beneath the strange plants the place is disorganized and untidy, with various objects—clothes and metal tools and open containers—lying sloppily around all over the place. Everything looks filthy.

Welcome. No need to be afraid or to scream. Please make yourselves comfortable.

It's like a voice coming from inside my head, and I slap my hands over my ears. At the same time, I know exactly where the voice is really coming from. It's coming from the other creatures, waiting for us in the center of the domed, jungly room.

They are shorter than the ones that brought us here and a whole lot uglier, because they are not even remotely humanoid. They basically consist of big, squashy heads, about three feet in diameter. Where the ears would be there are instead appendages like hands with three fat, blunt fingers. I don't even know if they have feet because the soft flesh of the heads lies in folds on the floor. They move by kind of oozing along, like slugs.

They don't have hair; they have things like droopy antennae. They have a row of protruding eyes, like frogs' eyes, that go all the way around; I can't tell how many. And below the eyes hang what must be mouths: wrinkled, permanently open orifices, with ropes of yellowish saliva dangling from top to bottom. The hands on the sides of the head are just long enough to reach into the mouths, and as they watch us they are constantly bending over, plucking wormlike things out of cylindrical containers full of liquid and sliding the wriggling creatures into their mouths.

Tim and I aren't paying a whole lot of attention to their polite welcome and the information that we don't need to be afraid. Just looking at them makes me feel like throwing up; I'm making a gagging noise of total horror and fear.

And then we both start screaming again when two of the tall ones take our arms and slide long needles into them. I can see the blood flowing out through a tube into a kind of plastic bag.

As soon as they have taken the blood, they remove the first needles and jab us with others. Now they are putting something in, instead of taking blood out. A sudden warmth flows through me and a feeling of calm. I know that somewhere inside I'm still as terrified as ever. But now I can relax; I can look around and see what's going on; I can think.

And, for the first time since this whole thing started, I can talk to Tim, who is standing next to me, still holding his portfolio. "Unbelievable," I say in an undertone. "Abducted by aliens—like those nuts are always blabbing about in the tabloids."

Tim has been injected too, but it doesn't seem to be working as well on him, maybe because he's so much heavier than me. His eyes are wide with fear; he is breathing loudly, barely under control. "But this is *real!*" he says, his voice high-pitched. "What are they doing to us? Are they going to let us out of here?"

We are glad you are feeling better now, the heads tell us. *Please sit down and make yourselves comfortable.*

It's an instruction, not an invitation, because the tall ones are already leading us to an object like a dirty recliner couch. I try not to think about what the stains on it might be. As soon as we sit down, cables secure us there; the part under our feet rises up, and the part under our heads falls back so that we are half sitting and half lying. We are trapped.

But because of the injection, I'm still not going nuts with fear and glad of it. "Did you hear what he said?" I ask the heads. "Why did you bring us here? What are you going to do with us? And are you going to let us go? We'd kind of like to go back."

We don't think *we are going to hurt you. We don't* think *we are going to keep you here. We just want to perform a few tests. Because of The Others, you see.*

"Gimme back my drawings!" Tim shrieks. The tall ones have taken his portfolio and brought it to the heads, who look through the drawings, paying no attention to Tim's screams.

Clearly, the heads are the ones in control, the tall ones their servants or slaves or robots—or their bodies. Because it is the tall ones who do things to us while the heads watch, slurping down their living snacks.

The tall ones clamp something around our heads, which buzzes and vibrates. The tall ones take grimy metal cylinders and slide them over our bodies while the heads look at patterns flashing across the domed ceiling. The tall ones make us spit into rubbery containers, which seal automatically, and give the containers to the heads. The tall ones use more needles to extract more blood, which they put into different containers and also give to the heads. The heads seem rather careless and sloppy, spilling our bodily fluids, the tall ones really doing all the work. I have no idea how long this is taking, and yet I'm not curious about the time and don't bother to look at my watch.

Fine. Very good. You will be taken back now, the heads say, meaning me. *And you we will keep,* they add, meaning Tim.

This news is too much for Tim to take, despite the drug. "You're keeping me here and letting him go?" Tim screams, struggling violently. "You can't do that! You have to let me go too! My career! Please, please let me go! I can't stand it if you keep me here! I'll kill myself first! I'll—"

The tall ones give him another shot, and he passes out.

"But you can't keep him here. You have to let him go too," I beg them. "What do you think will happen if he just disappears? You don't think people will be curious about it? I'll tell them everything, and then they'll

. . . they'll . . ." And then I can't think of what to say, because I know what people will think about me if I tell them any of this.

We must keep him, because of The Others. And somehow, I detect a note of fear in the voice at the mention of "The Others." *We will come back to the same place and find you there in exactly two days.*

"And the cops and the army will be waiting there for you!" I shout at them. The drug seems to be wearing off me too, at the thought of what they might possibly do to Tim. "You can't do this! I'll tell everybody! It's not fair! It's illegal!"

You will remember nothing. You will remember nothing at all.

Another needle pierces my arm.

CHAPTER TWO

I OPEN MY EYES, THEN SQUEEZE THEM SHUT against the glare of sunlight. I'm in an uncomfortable position, my limbs stiff, my skin filmed with sweat. I'm also very hungry. I slowly open my eyes again.

I'm sitting in the car, at the driver's seat, in bright daylight, on the empty stretch of road where I was driving Tim to catch the bus.

"Hey, what happ—" I start to say, turning to Tim.

Tim isn't there.

I sit up straighter, rubbing sweat off my forehead. The last thing I knew, I was driving Tim down this road in the darkness at 11:35 P.M. I look at my watch. It's 7:30 in the morning. And Tim isn't here.

Now I'm wide awake. . . A million worries flash through my mind. Why am I here? Why didn't we get to Bridgetown? How am I going to explain to my parents where I was with the car all night? What am I going to tell Tim's parents? Worst of all, what happened to Tim?

And why do I have no memory of the last eight hours?

I dash out of the car and run around, shouting Tim's name. I look for him on both sides of the road. There is no response and no sight of him. In about fifteen minutes I realize this is useless and slump back into the car.

The key is right there in the ignition. I start the car and drive slowly, not knowing what to do, still looking to see if Tim is anywhere around here. I'm completely confused; nothing like this has ever happened to me before. Was Tim kidnapped or something? What's happening to him right this minute? Is he still alive?

I pull over to the side of the road and check my wallet. The twenty-five dollars I had is still there, so I wasn't robbed. And if anybody had robbed Tim, wouldn't they have robbed me too and probably also stolen the car?

One thing I do know, suddenly, is that the sooner I get home, the sooner they'll be able to start seriously looking for Tim—if they aren't looking for us already. I make a U-turn and head quickly back.

I dread this confrontation with my parents, but there's no avoiding it. They'll be furious that I had the car out all night and didn't call them. And how are they going to take the crazy story that Tim disappeared and I don't remember anything about it?

As I drive I keep having the unreasonable hope that Tim somehow got back home. It's hard to believe he would just leave me there in the car, though. And it's even harder to believe that Tim, who is not exactly physically energetic, would have *walked* all the way home.

"Why didn't you *call* us?" Mom asks me. "We were so worried! How could you do this?"

"Just tell us where you really were all night, Leo," Dad says, his voice ominously quiet.

"I'm trying to tell you. I just kind of blacked out. I was driving with Tim on Route Thirty-eight to Bridgetown. That's the last thing I remember. He wanted to get away without his parents knowing. You know what they're like."

"We know them a lot better now," Dad coldly informs me. "We've been spending a lot of time on the phone with them for the last eight hours. They kept us up all night." Mom and Dad aren't eating breakfast, just drinking coffee, looking haggard.

"So they know he was with me?"

"That was the first thing they suspected. They made sure by calling everybody else they could think of," Dad tells me. "It got pretty obvious after a while that you were together, since you're best friends, and you had the car and had disappeared too. Is Tim trying to make them believe this same dumb story now about blacking out, losing his memory?"

"Er . . . I don't think so."

"What do you mean? He's telling them something

different?" Mom says, sounding bewildered. She's more worried than anything else, because she knows I never lie. Dad knows it too; he's just accusing me of lying because he's so angry. And I know what I'm telling them *does* sound pretty implausible.

"Uh, he's probably not telling them anything, because . . . well, I don't think he's home."

"*What?*" they both say at the same time.

I start to say we should call Tim's house right away and find out if he got home. Then I think about what it's going to be like to deal with his parents if he *isn't* home, which is the more likely possibility. "I . . . I was driving him to Bridgetown, to catch the midnight bus to New York. He had an appointment there this morning with a publisher—he sent them his drawings, and they were interested and wanted to talk to him. And you know his parents would never in a million years let him go. So I was helping him out—he figured it could be the beginning of his career. The last thing I remember, it was eleven thirty-five and we were driving on Route Thirty-eight. The next thing I remember is waking up there in the car at seven-thirty—and Tim wasn't anywhere around."

They just stare at me, not saying anything.

"I know it sounds crazy, but it's the truth!" I insist.

"You're sure about that, Leo? You're very, very sure?" Dad says, his eyes fixed on mine.

"Would I expect you to believe anything so crazy if

it *wasn't* the truth?" I ask him. I know it sounds lame. But the one thing I have going for me is that I've never lied to them before.

"I hope you're sure, because Tim's parents are going to be a lot more upset about this than we are if he's still not home."

I know that. I also know that Tim's parents are going to be a lot more suspicious of me than Mom and Dad, partly because they don't know me as well and partly because that's just the way they are. I feel more dread than ever as Dad gets up to go to the phone.

But as nervous as I am, I also feel something else—something I've been aware of ever since I woke up. "I'm starving," I say. "I've got to have something to eat, anything." I can't remember ever being this hungry in my life.

Dad makes the phone call. Tim isn't there. And as sick with worry as I am, I still keep gulping down more bread and peanut butter.

Of course we go to Tim's house, in case he calls or shows up or something. Two cops are already there when we arrive.

Both my parents are in jeans and T-shirts; Dad's unshaven; they clearly haven't had much sleep. But Tim's parents, who kept mine up all night, look like they're ready to go to a formal party. They've always been more conventional than my parents, but I've never before seen them dressed so immaculately in their own home. Tim's father is wearing a suit and tie; his mother has on stockings and high heels, and her face and hair look like she just got back from the beauty salon. "Good morning," Tim's mother says, in a flat, expressionless voice.

Her behavior is very odd. She doesn't seem the least bit upset that her son is missing. I knew she was a snob, but now she seems to have turned into an emotionless zombie.

The cops sit me down in a straight-backed dining room chair, which has been placed in the very center of their living room. The two cops and the two sets of parents are all staring at me. I feel like a prisoner being cross-examined.

I tell them exactly what happened, including Tim's plans about the publishing company. I know he wouldn't want me to tell his parents this, but that doesn't matter anymore. All that matters is doing everything I can to help them find Tim. The older and fatter of the two cops, Captain Kroll, seems to be in charge. He asks me questions about the exact location of the car and the time, and the other cop writes down my answers.

"And does this, uh, supposed publishing company have a name?" Tim's father asks me.

I tell him the name. On the one hand I'm reluctant, because I know he'll make trouble for them somehow—he's a lawyer; recently he's been doing a lot of work for the factory bosses in town, and he knows how to make trouble for people. But I have no choice, since it is one of the few things I'm telling them that can be verified. And maybe Tim is there!

Tim's father calls from the cellular phone he carries in the breast pocket of his suit jacket. He lifts his eyebrows when Directory Assistance gives him the number of the publishing company in New York, as though indicating surprise that anything I have said might be true.

He calls the company and asks about Tim, his face absolutely blank while he listens to the answer. "So you state that he did have an appointment with you at nine o'clock this morning and never showed up?" Tim's father says.

I glance over at Mom and Dad, slumping down in the chair with disappointment.

Tim's father listens on the phone a little while, then says, obviously interrupting the person on the other end, "Look, I don't need to hear about what you refer to as his 'talent.' The boy is a minor, and I consider it highly questionable of you to encourage these scribblings of his, which we, as his parents, have forbidden. Not to mention actually inviting him to your premises, in another state. You will be hearing from me."

He clicks off the phone and slips it back into his pocket, not looking at me, and turns to the older cop. "Well, I suppose this gives credence to his claim that Tim believed they were actually on their way for him to catch this bus. The next step is to find out what this person did with my son—and the three hundred and fifty-seven dollars he had on him."

"Hey, now wait just a minute," Dad says, leaning forward on the couch. It's practically the first thing he's said since we arrived. "Are you accusing Leo of theft and lying? Are you claiming he's responsible for Tim's disappearance?"

Tim's father ignores Dad, still talking to the cops. "This boy was the last person to see my son. And all he can come up with is that he passed out and remembers nothing." He shrugs slightly. "If we're going to find out what happened to my son and that three hundred and fifty-seven dollars, this person needs to be formally booked and subjected to more rigorous questioning."

Now Mom and Dad are both arguing with him. They know Tim is my best friend and I wouldn't hurt him or take his money. Mom and Dad know I don't lie, even though my story is full of holes.

Tim's father just shakes his head at them, looking disgusted. Tim's mother says nothing, sitting primly beside Tim's father. I can't believe she's continuing to be so unemotional about her son disappearing. Is she completely under the control of Tim's father? Or does she just care more about her clothes and her house and her social status than she does about her own son?

It's the older cop, Captain Kroll, who finally quiets Mom and Dad down. "Just hold on, hold on a minute," he says. "Don't worry, there's no cause for any criminal proceedings, not yet anyway."

"What?" For the first time Tim's father allows anger to show in his voice. "He goes off with my son—who had three hundred and fifty-seven dollars of my money on him—and comes back without him and says he has no memory of what happened. And you don't think—"

Captain Kroll lifts one hand. "Excuse me, sir, please," he says. "I'd agree with you too that it sounds very suspicious. Except . . ."

"Except what?" Tim's father demands.

"Except for certain other incidents, one over in Monroe County, the other out in the Westwood Park area. Two other incidents, not far from here, of people who lost certain amounts of time. Blanked out, amnesia, whatever. Responsible people, you might like to know, who had nothing to gain by telling these stories."

Captain Kroll gives Tim's father a long look—he doesn't seem to like him either!—then turns to me. "And these other stories were a lot like yours," he says in a more patient tone of voice. "People driving in an isolated area late at night who woke up later and didn't remember a thing. And in both those cases the police found one person who was able to help these people out. And maybe the same person could help you out too."

"Did anybody just disappear with cash in these other cases?" Tim's father demands.

Captain Kroll shakes his head. "No. But in both cases this person—a professional—helped the people to remember."

"To remember what happened when they blanked out?" I ask him.

"To remember what they thought happened during the time they lost," Captain Kroll says. "I'm not saying how much I believe in everything they said; this kind of stuff, I don't know." He sounds slightly embarrassed now. "But I do believe those people really did lose hours of time—for one thing, they didn't gain anything by it and were real inconvenienced, in fact—and I believe this young man here honestly lost hours of time too. And getting the help of this professional is one possible way of finding out some clues about what might have happened to your son. We'll be doing all the usual searches, sure, starting with a thorough check of the car. But there's no reason not to try this other way too; nothing to lose and maybe something to gain."

"What kind of, uh, professional is this you're talking about?" Mom says doubtfully.

"A health professional," Captain Kroll says. "A psychologist. An expert in hypnotism."

CHAPTER THREE

I'M ACTUALLY GLAD TO BE GOING TO THIS psychologist. I want to do anything I can to find out why I blanked out and what happened that I don't remember. And mainly I want to do anything I can to help Tim, as fast as possible. I know the longer a kid is missing, the less chance there is of finding him alive.

They discover nothing unusual or incriminating in the car. But Tim's father is very suspicious—and impatient. He's not happy Captain Kroll wouldn't book me. Mom and Dad and I all got the strong feeling that Tim's father is going to pull strings to go over Kroll's head and have me charged with some kind of criminal activity. We call the psychologist—Captain Kroll gave us his number—and tell the voice on the phone that this is very urgent. We get an appointment for early that evening.

There's something vaguely familiar about the name of this psychologist, Dr. Viridian, but I can't remember what it is. And I wonder why his office is located in the industrial area of town, where the air is so polluted.

Dr. Viridian is tall and good-looking, like a doctor

on TV, and has a smooth, soothing voice. He doesn't wear a lab coat or anything; he's casually dressed in expensive-looking clothes. His office is large, the furniture very plush and comfortable, in subdued, bland colors. He lets Mom and Dad stay at first, while I tell him what happened last night.

He listens carefully, nodding occasionally, his expression concerned and understanding. The questions he asks are so right on and acute that it almost seems like he knows what I'm going to say before I say it.

Mom notices too. "It sounds like you've seen many cases like this before, not just the two the police mentioned," she tells him when I've finished.

"Quite a few," he says, smiling slightly at her in a professional but warm way. "And I'd like to assure you right away that what this sounds like is in no way a mental illness. Fugal amnesia is not uncommon."

"Fugal amnesia?" Dad asks him.

"Fugal means running," the doctor says. "When something happens to a person that is too traumatic— too terrifying—for the conscious mind to tolerate, the mind runs away from the experience. It forgets it. That's how the mind protects itself from the horror it cannot live with."

Mom and Dad look pretty worried now. I feel a little shaky myself. What could have happened that was so terrible my mind had to run away from it? And what does that mean about what happened to Tim?"

"So we go beneath the conscious mind—into the unconscious," the doctor is explaining. "Hypnosis is how we get there. When the subject is in a hypnotic trance, the memory of the horror is released, brought out into the open."

"Yeah, but if what happened is so terrible that the conscious mind had to run away from it, then what happens to the, uh . . . subject when this terrible memory comes back?" I want to know.

"I understand your concern, and it is true that there is often some unpleasantness when the memory surfaces." (What exactly does he mean by "unpleasantness"? I wonder.) The doctor leans toward me. "But you must understand that you will be in a very deep state of relaxation—a state in which the memory can be faced and tolerated. I assure you, I have done this procedure over and over again, and the subject is always very much improved as a result."

Then Mom and Dad have to leave, looking back at me as they go out the door, as if they're really not so sure about this whole thing. But the cops recommended this guy, and he seems trustworthy and is obviously a successful psychologist. And what else can I do to help find Tim?

The doctor invites me to sit in a very comfortable reclining chair, and he sits down across from me. He presses a switch on the desk, and the lights in the room dim. He presses another switch, and I hear a faint whirring.

Then he begins speaking to me in a gentle but authoritative voice. "Your body is relaxing now. It is a soothing warmth that starts in your feet and moves up your legs, up your spine. Soon there will be no muscle tension anywhere in your body. And your mind is emptying. You are concentrating on my voice and nothing else. You have no worries, no other thoughts, only my voice. Soon you will be in a deep sleep, aware only of my voice . . ."

At first I resist, it seems so cornball. But gradually it actually starts to work . . . I begin to feel very relaxed and very sleepy. My mind is a blank.

"Are you asleep now?"

I nod.

"You are aware only of my voice?"

I nod again.

He pauses. Then he says brightly, like somebody talking to a little child, "You are three years old. It is your third birthday. Are you there?"

"Uh-huh," I say.

"Tell me what you see, what is happening."

And I tell him, in a baby voice, things I have not remembered for years. Mom and Dad and I are the only ones there. We are in a different house. I describe the room, the kitchen tablecloth, the cake, the presents. Dad has a beard; Mom has long hair. It's just like it's really happening again.

He takes me back to my first day of school. I am in

the classroom; I see the view out the window, and the teacher in her blue-and-white dress, and the kids who are crying because they don't want to be there. But I'm not crying; I'm eager and curious. I enjoy the games we play.

He takes me back to last night.

Tim and I are driving on Route 38 to Bridgetown. I'm nervous, afraid I'm going to get in trouble for this. We have a little argument because the car is acting funny, and Tim accuses me of not filling it up, and I call him fatso. And then . . .

"I can't see what happens next," I say. "Something's in the way."

"You are more relaxed now," the doctor tells me. "More deeply asleep. You are perfectly safe. Nothing can harm you now. You are driving with Tim. You have a little argument. And then . . ."

I tell him about the strange lights that Tim points out to me. The doctor asks me to describe them in complete detail, and I do. I tell him that right after we see the lights, the car dies. We are stuck there in the darkness.

My mind goes blank again. The doctor instructs me to relax even more; he tells me I can remember everything now; I am perfectly safe.

I'm moaning now, my head rolling back and forth on the soft chair. "Oh, it's so horrible! The scariest thing that ever happened to me. Oh, my God! It's impossible; I can hardly believe it. But it's really happening. I can't stand it!"

The doctor has to spend a few minutes calming me down. And then I tell him a very strange story. The noises on the windows, the lapping on my neck, the undulating creatures we can't run away from, taking us to the lights, being strapped in, going up so fast, up to the big jungly ship. The tall ones, the heads, the way they take our blood right away, the other things they do to us. It's a real effort for me to keep from screaming. The doctor has to stop many times to soothe me.

He also asks me lots of questions. He wants to know absolutely every detail. And I remember every detail—what the creatures looked like and smelled like, the messy alien ship, the weird plants, the stuff lying around on the floor, the needles, the machines, the way they look at Tim's drawings, exactly what we say to each other. Every time I skip over something or don't describe it completely, the doctor presses me for more details.

"These creatures you describe as the heads," he says. "You say they mentioned something they called The Others. What exactly did they say about them?"

"Not much. . . . They only mentioned them twice. The first time, they said they had to do the tests on us because of The Others. Then later they said they had to keep Tim because of The Others."

"I see. That was why they had to keep Tim. . . ." He pauses. "Did they explain?"

"No. They just said they had to keep him because of The Others."

"That was all they said about them? Nothing else?"

"Nothing."

He leads me through the rest of the story. Again, he questions me very closely when I get to the part when the heads say they will come back to the same place in exactly two days. We go over this several times.

Then they give me the last injection, which is some drug that seems to have totally destroyed my memory, because we can't get anything else until I wake up the next morning in the car, the part I consciously remember.

The doctor calms me down again. Yeah, I'm relaxed, but I'm sweating, and I also feel like screaming. Going through this experience has been really unpleasant. But after he instructs me to relax again, I begin to feel a little better.

And then, for a while, the doctor says nothing. I am vaguely aware of him pressing a button on his desk and the whirring noise stopping. He gets up and removes things and inserts things into some kind of machine. Then he just sits there. I don't know why he's keeping me here now, while he just seems to be thinking, but I don't care, because I am in a very deep trance. I just wait.

Finally the doctor says, "You must listen to me very closely now. This is the most important part." The doctor's voice has changed. It is less soothing, and there is a commanding, forceful tone to it. "What you have just told me," he says, very slowly and distinctly, "is a false memory."

"False?" I say, feeling uncomfortable in a different way now. Because this memory that he has just dredged out of me, incredible as it is, seems absolutely real to me. I know it is exactly what happened.

"It is false," Dr. Viridian says, with total conviction. "It was implanted in your brain to cover up what really happened."

"But . . . but you just helped me remember it all," I say, feeling more uncomfortable than ever. I'm in a deep trance; I'm under the control of this guy, but a corner of my mind is still able to doubt. "Are you telling me that none of this happened at all? How do you know? And how do we find out what really happened, so we can help Tim?"

"I am here to help you," the doctor says, his voice soothing again. "The more you relax, the more I can help you find out what really happened and find Tim. You are so relaxed that you do not question me. That is the only way I can help you. Are you more relaxed now?"

"Yes," I say, so relaxed I can barely get the word out.

"You are so relaxed now that you can't move. Can you move your arms, your legs, any part of your body?"

I try to move, and I can't. I can't even move my mouth to answer his question.

He kneels down and very quickly injects something into my arm. Then he waits. And while he waits, I feel my consciousness shrinking, shrinking, until the only entrance into my mind is a tiny pinhole. And soon that pinhole is filled by the doctor's voice.

"Concentrate," Dr. Viridian says. "You will forget everything you have just told me about last night; you will forget everything about The Others. And this is what you will remember. This is what is real."

Except it's not just a voice; it's more than that. It's a story, a memory: I am being reminded of the true events of last night—as true as my third birthday and my first day of school.

Then we wait for a while.

Dr. Viridian presses a button on his desk, and a whirring noise begins. He asks me questions. I am in a deep trance.

Now I remember what really happened last night. I tell him.

Chapter Four

THE LIGHT IS ON, AND I AM SITTING UP IN A regular chair when Dr. Viridian buzzes his receptionist and tells her to send Mom and Dad back into the consultation room.

"Leo, are you all right?" Mom says as soon as she sees me, looking quickly over at the doctor, then back to me again.

"Yeah, I'm all right," I say. "A little shaken up, but okay. I think you two, uh, better sit down."

"Did you get your memory back?" Dad wants to know.

"Well, yeah," I say evasively. I look over at the doctor. I feel weird about telling them what I remember about last night. And I'm sure the doctor is more experienced than I am about breaking this kind of news to people.

"When the officer told you I had helped those other people, did he happen to mention to you what kinds of things they remembered under hypnosis?" the doctor asks Mom and Dad.

"No, he didn't," Dad says.

"But there *was* something a little odd, now that I think of it," Mom says. "He said he wasn't sure he believed in that kind of stuff, something like that, even though it seemed to help the people." She frowns. "Do you know what he meant? Does it have something to do with what Leo remembered?" She turns to me again, looking worried.

"What those other people remembered—and what Leo remembers—is being abducted by aliens. I'm sure you've heard about this phenomenon."

Now they both look stricken. For a moment they don't know what to say. I don't blame them. It's just about the same as if the doctor told them I'm certifiably insane.

"Leo!" Dad says, sounding a little angry. "Don't tell me! Is *that* what you're claiming happened last night?"

"I'm not claiming anything," I say. "The doctor hypnotized me. And while I was hypnotized, what I remembered was, uh, pretty weird. And I still remember it now."

"Tim's father is gonna *love* this," Dad says, rolling his eyes.

"I can understand your skepticism," the doctor says. "But what you may not realize is that great numbers of people have experienced very similar memories. So many—and so similar—that their reports are now being studied by serious scientists, myself included. So I urge you, try to approach this with open minds. One of the main problems these people have is that they are treated with such contempt and scorn by the rest of the world—including their own families. Please, don't make it harder on Leo than it already is."

The doctor's tone is so kind and gentle and reasonable that I can tell Mom and Dad feel a little bit chastened. I'm grateful to him for trying to make it easier for me. I'm also pretty skeptical about these "memories" myself—even though, as crazy as they are, they *feel* like real memories.

I tell Mom and Dad about the bright flashing lights in the sky and the car breaking down. I tell them about the little greenish men with big eyes, powerfully strong, who wrestled Tim and me from the car and into their vehicle. I tell them about the spaceship they took us to, gleaming and futuristic. I tell them about the leader of the little greenish men, the captain, who explained to us that—

"They spoke English?" Dad interrupts me. "They could breathe our atmosphere?"

"I'm just telling you what I remember!" I say, feeling like an idiot.

"Sorry," Dad says, glancing over at the doctor, then back to me. "Go on."

I tell them how the captain explained they were here to help us save our planet from being destroyed by political violence and corruption. How he explained that they have to be very careful and secretive about making contact with us, because if everybody knew about them, then they might have the wrong kind of effect on our civilization—like the way Europeans obliterated whole cultures when they invaded the new world. What they are doing is selecting certain individuals and training them to be able to help save the world in a way that will seem natural. And Tim was chosen to be one of those individuals. "He said they'd return him in a week," I finish.

"They picked *Tim* to save the world?" Dad says, and I can tell he'd be laughing if he weren't so upset by my craziness. "And they're going to train him how to do it in one week?"

"I have a reading list here," the doctor says, taking a printed sheet from his desk and handing it to Dad. "It might help you understand a little better."

"Thanks." Dad takes it and folds it up and shoves it in his pocket without looking at it. "And thanks for helping Leo get his memory back. How much is all this help going to cost me?"

"Seventy-five dollars," the doctor says.

Dad silently writes out a check and hands it to him.

"If you have any more problems, Leo, I'm always here to help you," the doctor says.

I thank him—even though I hope I'll never be seeing him again.

Mom and Dad and I are very thoughtful. Nobody talks until we're in the car and Mom says, "Oh, could we stop at the supermarket on the way home? I just need to pick up a couple of things. It'll only take a minute."

"I can't wait until Tim's father hears about this," Dad mutters.

I sigh. "Look, I'm sorry; I can't help it. Those are the memories that came back when I was hypnotized. I think it's as crazy as you do."

And then, in the supermarket, I pick up a tabloid newspaper as I'm waiting with Mom in the checkout line. And I just happen to notice an advertisement near the back—it catches your attention because there's a heavy black line around it:

AMNESIA? BLACKOUTS? UNEXPLAINED LOST TIME? UNUSUAL SIGHTINGS AT NIGHT? THESE MAY ALL BE INDICATIONS THAT YOU HAVE HAD A SPECIAL ENCOUNTER. FOR EXPERIENCED AND SPECIALIZED PROFESSIONAL HELP, CONTACT DR. VIRIDIAN.

Directly underneath it is another ad:

ANY PEOPLE WHO HAVE HAD THE ABOVE EXPERIENCES, PATIENTS OF DR. VIRIDIAN OR OTHERS, WHO WOULD LIKE TO GET TOGETHER AND SHARE OUR EXPERIENCES, PLEASE CALL ANNABELLE KINCAID . . .

I can hardly believe it, it's such a strange coincidence. Mom is preoccupied with paying for the groceries, so I wait until we're back in the car to read the two ads to them. "I thought I'd heard his name before, and this is probably where," I tell them.

"So that's the scientific level this guy's at," Dad says. "He advertises in the tabloids."

"Yeah, and then I remember about little green men. It's so *boring*—just what you'd expect to see in the tabloids. Why didn't I remember something more . . . scientific?" I think for a moment. "But isn't it interesting that Dr. Viridian's patients want to get together and talk about what happened to them?" I say.

Dad and Mom look at each other. "I just wish we hadn't listened to that cop," Dad says. "Seventy-five bucks that guy Viridian charged me, and all we find out is that you remember being abducted by aliens like from a third-rate movie."

"And it didn't do anything to help find Tim," I say. I'm worried about him. But I'm also kind of excited about the idea of contacting these other patients of Dr. Viridian's and trying to find out more about him.

Except that it's beginning to get dark now. I start to feel nervous. I don't like being in the car at night—and I've never felt that way before. Does that mean what I remembered is real? I feel very relieved when we get home.

Until we listen to the message on the answering machine. It's from Tim's father. At first I'm hoping he's going to tell us they found Tim. But he doesn't say anything about the search, which obviously means they haven't found him. He just says I have to be at police headquarters tomorrow at 10 A.M. for further questioning. A police car will pick me up at 9:30.

I groan. "What am I going to tell them?" I say.

Nobody knows. It's clear to all of us that if I tell them what I remembered under hypnosis, they'll think I'm lying or that I'm crazy.

"Well, the one thing in your favor is that the doctor *was* recommended by Captain Kroll," Mom says. "That might give you a tiny bit of credibility."

"It would be even better if the doctor was there," I say. "Then they'd have more proof that there are other people who had experiences like I did and memories like mine. I wonder if he'd do it?"

"Sure he would—for a price," Dad says.

"Oh, come on," Mom says hotly. "Don't be like Tim's father. Who cares what it costs if it's going to help Leo—and Tim?"

"Sorry. You're right," Dad says. He calls the doctor and leaves a message on his machine that I need his help at the police station tomorrow, that it's urgent because of Tim being missing and that of course he will be compensated for it.

I'm more worried than ever about Tim, since they haven't found him yet, and apprehensive about the next day. I'm tired and go to bed early. I have trouble sleeping at first, worrying about what's going to happen tomorrow. The doctor probably won't get the message in time or won't be able to change his schedule. And then I'll be on my own, with nothing to tell them except this dumb story about little green men and nobody to back me up about it.

But finally I fall asleep. . . . I am dreaming that Tim and I are strapped to something like an operating table. Creatures with long arms and tiny heads are doing things to us with weird instruments, poking and prodding us and sticking things into us. There are other creatures there too, really gross, like big, squashy heads, who keep eating living things like worms. They seem to be afraid of something they call The Others. They mention them several times. And then they keep Tim! They say they'll bring him back in two days, but why should I believe them? They give me another shot. They warn me again about The Others. Then they take me back to the car.

What if they come back to get me again? I wake up in the middle of the night, terrified, moaning.

And with no memory of what I was dreaming.

Chapter Five

I DON'T TELL MOM AND DAD THAT I WOKE UP from a terrible nightmare—a nightmare that I can't remember at all. I don't want them to get the idea that I might really be crazy.

We call the doctor several times before 9:30 but only get his taped message, even after 9:00. It's very odd. Even if the doctor *is* coming to the police station—or out doing something else—you'd think his receptionist would be at the office to make appointments. Why isn't she there?

Dad can't come to the police station; he can't skip another day of work. At least Mom gets the day off again, so she can come with me. Before Dad goes to work, we talk about what I should say. Of course, if the doctor is there, I'll have to tell them what happened at his office, even though it sounds so crazy. So we figure I have no choice but to tell them the same story, even if the doctor isn't there, so that we can get him to back it up later.

Mom and Dad keep telling me everything will be fine, don't worry, there is no evidence against me, nothing they can do to hurt me. But before Dad goes to work, he tells us to phone him if anything goes slightly wrong—which means they really are worried too.

I am watching from the window when the police car pulls up a little before 9:30. We don't wait for them to come and ring the bell; we walk out as soon as I see the car.

One cop gets out of the car as we are coming down the walk. He asks me my name. He doesn't touch me, but he is very close behind us as we walk to the car and get into the backseat.

I'm disappointed that Captain Kroll isn't here, since he knows about Dr. Viridian and seemed a little sympathetic toward me yesterday. I can only hope he will be at the police station when they question me. These two guys are young and strongly built and have guns. Why did they send *two* armed cops to drive us to the station? Did they think I was going to try to run away?

They don't say a word as we drive, and Mom and I don't talk either. I keep telling myself not to hope that the doctor will be at the station—the message probably came too late for him to be able to change his schedule.

And what will happen if I can't convince them that I'm innocent? Mom and Dad told me not to worry, but what do they know? They're not lawyers like Tim's father. Is it possible that they could really lock me up?

The two cops take us to a dingy, windowless room with a long, plastic-topped table and then leave. I see immediately that the doctor isn't there. I tell myself not to hope that he might show up later.

Tim's father is there, of course, but not his mother. I'm very relieved to see that Captain Kroll and the other cop who was with him at Tim's house are sitting at the table too. There is also a senior cop with a very large badge, who exudes an air of self-importance. The other man at the table is wearing a business suit and is very well groomed. Is he a lawyer or what? Nobody tells us. Finally, there is a woman who takes notes. And the younger cop from the day before also tapes the proceedings.

The man in the business suit does the questioning. He is not impolite, but he is very businesslike and does not smile. I start out by telling the same story I told them yesterday, exactly what I remembered before going to the doctor. When I get to the part about the publishing company, I stop and ask Tim's father, "Did you call them again?"

"We're the ones who are asking the questions," Tim's father says.

"Okay, but maybe he showed up there later than he expected. Maybe he—"

"If he were there, we wouldn't need to be doing this, would we?" the man in the suit says. "Just go on with your story, please."

I sigh and continue. I tell them about the little argument with Tim and how, after that, I blanked out and didn't remember anything until the next morning and ran around looking for Tim and checked my wallet and then drove home. "At least, that's all I remembered yesterday," I add.

"I see. Your memory has improved since then," Tim's father says sarcastically.

The man in the suit gives him a look, and Tim's father snaps his mouth shut. "Can you explain what you mean by that?" the man in the suit asks me.

"This officer here"—I nod at Captain Kroll—"told us the name of a doctor, a psychologist, who specializes in people who have memory lapses. You said there were several other cases around here similar to this one, right?"

"Yes, there were," Captain Kroll agrees.

"But not with missing persons—and money," Tim's father puts in.

The man in the suit gives him another look and then says to me, "Please continue with what you were saying."

I tell them we went to Dr. Viridian and what he said about fugal amnesia and hypnosis. I tell them that he hypnotized me and that under hypnosis I had a memory of what happened during the time I blanked out—a memory that was still very clear after he woke me up. Then I hesitate.

"Yes? Will you tell us what you remember?"

I glance over at Mom, then back to the man in the

suit. "I know it sounds crazy, but it's what I remember. The doctor said he has many patients who have similar memories and that there are scientists who take these people's memories very seriously. We left the doctor a message to come here today but . . . I guess he couldn't make it."

"We'd just like to know what you remember, please."

I feel horribly embarrassed, but I know I have to tell them. Even if the doctor doesn't show up today, I'm sure they'll ask him about it later, to check my story out. Anyway, there is nothing else I *can* tell them. I tell them about the little greenish men and the spaceship and how they are trying to save the world, but they have to be secretive about it, so they train Earth people to do it. And that's why they're keeping Tim, and they'll bring him back in a week.

I very deliberately avoid looking at Tim's father while I'm telling this story; I don't want to see whatever obnoxious reaction he's having. The man in the suit remains expressionless, occasionally asking me for details in a blank voice. There is a long silence when I finish.

Then Tim's father bursts out with, "Do you honestly expect us to believe this ridiculous, transparent—"

"You know this is all on the record," the man in the suit interrupts him.

But Tim's father just laughs and shrugs. "Fine. Great. It's on the record that my son was taken away by little green men." And then he suddenly becomes very serious and leans toward me and says, "It's also on the record that this delinquent is blatantly trying to perpetrate a hoax, to cover up what he *really* did to my son!"

Now I'm angry too. "Tim is my best friend! Why would I do anything to hurt him?"

"He had three hundred and fifty-seven dollars on him," Tim's father says. "And you were the last person who saw him."

"If I wanted three hundred and fifty-seven dollars, I wouldn't get it by robbing my best friend and then dumping him somewhere and then coming back and telling everybody I was with him. That's crazy! And anyway, in case the rest of you don't know it, Tim outweighs me by about fifty pounds. Right?" I ask Tim's father.

"Uh . . . yes, I'd say that's accurate," he says a little stiffly.

"Look," I say. "All I want is to find Tim. Why else do you think I went to that doctor? Why else do you think I'd . . . embarrass myself by telling everybody here this crazy story I'm remembering now? And you can ask the doctor about it. He said a lot of people remember being abducted by aliens. And that's what I remember." I look around the table, breathing heavily. Even Tim's father doesn't say anything. Now I'm beginning to sympathize with all those people who have memories like I do—who I used to think were crazy. "Why don't you call Dr. Viridian?" I say to the man in the suit. "I have his number, and so does Captain Kroll."

They have a speakerphone here, so that everybody in the room can hear both sides of the conversation and it can be recorded. The man in the suit calls Dr. Viridian's number. But it doesn't ring. There are three tones, and then a taped voice says, "We are sorry. This number has been permanently disconnected."

Tim's father sits back in his chair and crosses his arms.

"But that's crazy!" I say. "We were just at his office yesterday. He told me he would be there if I needed his help. And we called him several times this morning and got his message."

"That's true, we did," Mom says.

"I know this doctor has a good reputation," Captain Kroll says. "Other districts have sent people to him. Maybe you could try again. I mean, in case you might have dialed wrong."

He tries two more times. There is the same taped response.

"Well, whatever happened to that doctor, I think what Leo is saying makes sense," Captain Kroll says. "Why would he attack and dispose of his best friend and then come back and say he was just with him? It sounds to me like there's a third party involved, someone who attacked them and didn't want Leo to remember what—"

"This is not the time for speculation. We're just looking for facts now," the man in the suit says. He looks around at the others. "And it seems to me we've collected all the facts we can from Leo today. You're free to go. But don't leave town. We may need you at any time for further questioning."

Tim's father doesn't say anything then. But as we're on our way out of the building, he comes up to Mom and me and says in an undertone, "Don't think you're off the hook. I'll get you for this, I promise you that." And he strides away.

"He's nuts," Mom whispers. "He has a problem, and all he can think of to do is take it out on somebody else."

I agree. He's scary. I wonder what he's going to do next, and when.

But at least I'm not in trouble with the cops, for the time being, anyway. It's still only noon when we get home, and Mom goes off to work for the afternoon.

Which leaves me alone and free to call the woman who put that ad in the paper about Dr. Viridian's patients getting together. I'm more curious than ever, now that Dr. Viridian has vanished.

Chapter Six

I FEEL A LITTLE LITTLE NERVOUS ABOUT MAKING THIS call. Who are these people, anyway? I can sense that Mom and Dad don't want me to get involved. But what can I lose by just calling?

I call the number in the ad. A woman's voice answers.

"May I speak to Annabelle Kincaid, please?" I feel my pulse picking up.

"Speaking."

"Oh, hello. My name is Leo Kasden. I saw your ad in the paper. I had one of those experiences too, and I went to Dr. Viridian about it. And I was hoping to find somebody else who might have had a similar experience."

"I'm glad you called. Viridian's always talking about how it's not an uncommon experience. Then you ask him to introduce you to some of his other patients, maybe form a support group, so you can have somebody to share it with, because nobody else understands. But helpful Dr. Viridian won't help you there. Suddenly it's all confidential, professional ethics, whatever. The

ad worked better than I expected. Got nine people coming tonight. You'll be ten, if you can make it."

"These are all people who were . . . abducted?" I ask
her.

There's a pause. "I thought you said you were too,"
she says suspiciously.

"Well, yes. I mean, I . . ."

"How old are you, anyway?"

"Sixteen."

"Oh, I get it. So you're a little shy," she says. "Well,
you don't need to be. You're welcome to come." She
gives me an address and directions. "See you at eight
o'clock tonight," she says.

I quickly thank her and tell her good-bye and hang
up.

It's odd that Dr. Viridian refused to organize a support group. Why doesn't he want his patients to talk to
each other?

Mom and Dad are hesitant, but they can't come up
with any reason why I shouldn't go. And then I realize
what's really bothering them. They're worried about me
driving alone in the car at night, afraid I might black
out again.

I'm worried about it too. It's only about ten miles to
this person's house, but the drive scares me. I almost
consider asking Mom or Dad to come with me—except
I'm sure the people at this meeting won't want intrud-
ers there who didn't have the experience they did. And

anyway, I refuse to be crippled by this irrational fear. After supper, I get in the car and go.

I drive as fast as I can, keeping my eyes on the road and avoiding looking at the sky. I'm afraid I might actually *see* some lights in the sky; I'm worried that the car might break down again. My hands are slippery with sweat on the steering wheel, even though I have the air-conditioning on.

Nothing happens on the way there. I find the address in about half an hour.

But as I walk toward the house I'm still apprehensive about driving back, when it will be later.

A fat woman answers the door. She's middle-aged, wearing tight pants and a lot of makeup, and she has long hair, like a teenager. She's holding a cigarette. "Hi, I'm Annabelle," she says. "You must be Leo, right?"

"Yes. Nice to meet you."

"Come on in. Everybody else is here."

There are about ten people sitting around in a small living room, which has fake wood paneling, a shag wall-to-wall carpet, maple furniture, and family photographs on the walls. Folding chairs have been moved in from another room, so there will be enough places to sit. Everybody introduces themselves, but I forget most of their names right away.

I'm the youngest one there; all the others look like they're thirty or older. There are four women, including Annabelle. Two of the men are wearing suits; everyone else is dressed more casually. Some of them, including me, seem a little shy or uncomfortable about being there.

One of the men in a suit already seems to have taken charge. His name is Herman. "Annabelle says you're a patient of Dr. Viridian's too," he says to me as I sit down in a folding chair. "That makes five of us here."

"Well, I saw him once, yesterday. But I don't think I'll be seeing him again. You know his phone's been disconnected?"

"Yeah, we know," Herman says.

"I had an appointment with him today," a thin, tense woman says. "The office was locked, no name on the door, nothing. Now I don't know who I'm going to go to for therapy. I keep having these . . . these awful dreams, you see."

"It's okay, honey," Annabelle comforts her. "That's what this meeting is all about—to help each other. Maybe some people have other therapists they can recommend."

"Yes, well, we might as well get started," Herman says. "We all tell each other our experiences, agreed?" People nod and murmur assent. "I'll be happy to go first, to break the ice," Herman volunteers. Nobody argues with him.

Herman had his first experience several months ago, when he was driving alone at night. He saw the lights in the sky before he blacked out. He woke up in the car the next morning. Someone he knew told him about Dr. Viridian's ad—Herman doesn't admit to reading that particular tabloid himself. Dr. Viridian explained the procedure and hypnotized him, and then it all came back.

"The car died, and then before I knew it there were all these little purple guys with big eyes," Herman says. "I tried to run away, but they pointed this ray gun thing at me, and then I had to do what they said. We rode up in this thing like a transparent bubble to their ship, a big saucer. All kinds of shiny, futuristic machinery. I have to admit, I was really scared. But they promised they wouldn't hurt me. They were just doing tests— scientists studying the human race. There was a thing kind of like an X-ray machine; they stuck things into my body; they did all kinds of stuff. They made me forget everything before they brought me back. A couple months later, same thing happened again."

"It happened more than *once*?" I ask him, thinking of the drive home.

"Uh-huh. Blacked out the second time too. So back I go to Dr. Viridian. Same story came out. The aliens just did more tests. Didn't hurt me, though. Hasn't happened again since, knock on wood. But . . . I keep wondering if they'll come back—and when."

A lot of people talk at once, agreeing with this. It seems that a fear of the experience recurring is quite common.

The five people who didn't go to Dr. Viridian went to someone named Pierce. I listen to the other people tell their stories, and I tell mine. At first it seems to me that all the stories are different. Sometimes the little men are orange; sometimes they're blue; sometimes they glow in the dark. They take some people from their cars, like me, but other people were actually taken from their houses. The tests they do on the people seem different too—at first. And the aliens give a variety of reasons for being here. Sometimes, as in my case, they are here to save the Earth. Other times they are scientists studying our species. Sometimes they are explorers, who simply ask questions.

But as more people tell their stories, I begin to see that they are really not so different after all. Everybody's aliens are different colors and have different features. But they are all humanoid, and they are all short; all, in other words, similar to the traditional "little green men" of the tabloids.

I think about the bizarre creatures in our own oceans on Earth—octopi and giant worms and things—how different they are from us. So why are all these aliens from other planets so ordinary, like little people? It's the same thing that bothered me about my own memories, and now it bothers me even more.

The interiors of the spaceships and what the aliens do to the human subjects also vary in specific details. And yet all the spaceships are gleaming and futuristic, like the spaceships on TV shows everybody has seen. And although everybody is terrified by the experience, the aliens are never cruel or threatening; they never want to take over the Earth or hurt the human race. Their motivations, though they vary from case to case, are always benign or scientific.

And the more I hear, the more skeptical I become.

I keep thinking "traditional"; I keep thinking "derivative." There is nothing truly weird or unexpected, nothing that everybody hasn't heard before—nothing that would require much imagination or skill to make up. Yet at the same time, the specific details are all slightly different. No two people were taken by exactly the same aliens.

The people in this room seem to have been abducted by ten *different* species of aliens. And yet each species of aliens is like something from a cheap comic book.

And the overall effect of hearing all these stories together is that I don't believe any of them. In fact, if someone's intention was to concoct a group of stories on purpose so that they would *not* be believed, this would be exactly the way to go about it. Nobody believed my story when I told it at the police station this morning.

And yet all these people really did have amnesia—they lost hours of time, which in every case can be verified. All of these people got back their memories—these memories that sound like they were *designed* not to be believed—when they were hypnotized by Viridian or Pierce.

The more I think about it, the more eerie it seems, and the more frightened I get. It's like a conspiracy. It seems clear to me that the real motivation of the hypnotists is not to bring out these people's true memories; their motivation is to cover up what *really* happened to them when they had amnesia.

And the scary part is, what *is* it that the hypnotists are working so hard to cover up?

Do I dare to suggest this idea, in order to find out if anybody else has noticed it too? Most of these people seem so fervent in their beliefs of what happened to them. What will their reaction be if I, the youngest one here, tell them they've probably all been duped?

But I have to. I have no choice. I may never see any of these people again. This is probably my only chance to find somebody else who sees the same sinister pattern I do. And I want to find somebody else because it's too frightening to understand it alone.

We've all told our stories now. Everyone is just sitting around talking to each other. "Excuse me, Herman," I say.

He glances over at me.

"Could you try to get everybody's attention again, please? There's something really important I need to say."

It takes Herman a little while, but finally he gets the people to quiet down. "Yes, what is it, Leo?" he says. They are all looking at me.

I try to explain my idea to them, hesitant at first. "Isn't it peculiar that there are *ten* different species of aliens? Wouldn't it make more sense if some of us were abducted by the same species? And isn't it peculiar that all our memories are like something we could have seen on a TV series or read in the newspaper?"

Nobody says anything for a moment. Then Herman sits up straighter in his chair and says, "What are you getting at, boy? Are you trying to say we're imagining these memories—just like everybody else thinks?"

"No, no, that's exactly the opposite of what I mean," I say very quickly, before the babble can break out again. "I'm not saying something didn't really happen to all of us; I'm not saying we weren't really abducted by aliens. What I'm saying is that I think the doctors took away our real memories and gave us these other stories. They did it so that no one would believe us and so that no one—including *us*—would know what really *did* happen to us."

Again, no one speaks for a moment. I hurry up and continue. "I mean, isn't it peculiar that when Annabelle arranged this meeting, Dr. Viridian disappears? Maybe he was afraid that once we all heard each other's stories, we might figure out he was up to something. Why wouldn't he talk to the police to try to help find Tim?

And what about Dr. Pierce? When was the last time anybody saw him?"

No one has seen him for several days.

"Maybe somebody should try to call him, just to see," I suggest. "By the way, where is his office?"

"In the industrial zone," says one of the women.

"So was Dr. Viridian's," I say. "It's interesting that these two doctors who treat people who were abducted both have their offices in the most polluted part of town."

"I'll call Dr. Pierce now." The woman picks up the phone, dials, and listens. Then she hangs up and turns and looks at me. "Permanently disconnected," she says quietly.

I leave soon after that, surer than ever that the hypnotists are trying to cover up what really happened to us. I'm just as scared as I was on the way here. As I start to drive, I tell myself it will be quicker going home, because I know the way.

Except, I suddenly realize, I'm not driving home. A cold panic creeps over me. I'm taking a complicated route in this unfamiliar neighborhood. At each intersection, I know whether to go left or right or straight ahead. Somehow I am compelled to do this; I have no choice.

Now my pulse is racing; I'm sweating more than ever; I feel like screaming. Is this some kind of posthypnotic suggestion? I'm completely conscious, yet I can do nothing to control the route I'm taking. Where am I going? This is a nightmare.

And it gets even more terrifying when I begin to notice that the big van behind me is making all the same turns I am.

I drive faster, making an effort to keep my hands from shaking on the wheel. The green van drives faster too. It doesn't seem to be trying to catch up with me or force me off the road. It just stays close behind me, following every move I make.

And then I turn left and I really do scream. Because now I recognize where I am.

I'm heading toward Bridgetown on Route 38.

Chapter Seven

Except for the green van behind me, the road is deserted—just like it was two nights ago when I was driving this way with Tim. There are no houses or factories or gas stations on this stretch of road, no place to stop and try to get help. Not that I *could* stop. Whatever is controlling me won't let me.

I remember what Herman and some of the other people at the meeting said about being abducted more than once. I know that's what's happening to me. I keep getting closer and closer to the place where I woke up yesterday morning. At any moment the car's going to break down. And then the little green men will come and overpower me and—

But those little green men were a false memory, planted in my mind by Dr. Viridian. The meeting tonight convinced me of that—and now I am being brought back here in only two days, when in the false memory the aliens said they'd be back in a week. So the benign little green men in their antiseptic spaceship isn't what's going to happen. Something unknown is going to happen—something my conscious brain ran away from.

Maybe something a lot worse than what the doctor got me to remember under hypnosis.

And then, ahead of me, someone is waving frantically at me from the side of the road. It's Tim. There's something different about him, but things are too crazy right now for me to pinpoint exactly what it is, and there's no doubt in my mind that it's him. And now, suddenly, I'm in control of what I'm doing. I brake as fast as I safely can, hoping the van isn't going to rear-end me.

I'm going too fast to be able to stop exactly where Tim is; I pull over about ten yards ahead of him. He is already running for my car, clutching his portfolio.

Someone from the van is running after him—or maybe more than one person; it's hard to tell. I push open the passenger door and Tim hurls himself inside, shouting in an oddly deep voice, "Get away from here! Hurry!"

Dr. Viridian is outside, reaching for Tim's portfolio. Tim slams his door shut. Dr. Viridian whips his hand away just in time to keep it from getting caught in the door. I swerve onto the road. "What's going on?" I ask Tim, turning toward him.

He doesn't answer, slumping back in the seat.

Dr. Viridian must have rushed back to the van, because it's already pulling out onto the road. It's going really fast now, not just following, but desperately trying to catch up with us. I floor the accelerator, but the van is getting closer.

Tim is still just sitting there with his eyes closed.

"Tim! What is—" I start to ask him again.

And then, in the rearview mirror, I see the van's headlights blink out. It stops moving. In a few seconds it's far behind us.

"What happened? Why did the van die? Where *were* you? What's going on?" I ask Tim, continually turning to look at him, then back to the road.

He doesn't answer me, lolling back in the seat, gasping for breath, his portfolio in his lap. I can't see him very well because it's so dark outside the car. But now that the van isn't chasing us and I can concentrate on studying him a little more closely, it suddenly hits me exactly what it is that's different about him. I look quickly away from him, feeling sick to my stomach and chills on the back of my neck at the same time.

Tim is taller than he was two days ago and thinner. His shirt is loose on him, but the sleeves are too short, and the bottom barely reaches his waist.

He still isn't saying anything. I take a couple of deep breaths and force myself to look back at him. There's no doubt about it. He's taller. He's lost a lot of weight. His nose is more prominent. I remember his oddly deep voice when he was shouting at me just now. I'm not imagining this. Tim is older.

I turn away from him again. I don't know what to say to him. I keep driving, feeling panicky, not thinking about where I'm going.

Finally Tim rolls his head over on the seat and says,

in his new deep voice, "The Others. Why you bring The Others? Why you tell them? Not supposed to."

"The Others?"

"The ones in van. Very dangerous. And now they saw what I look like." His voice is husky, like someone who just woke up, but there is also that tone of whining complaint in it. "You made bad mistake, Leo."

All at once I'm angry. "*I* made a mistake? I didn't do anything except what . . . what whoever delivered you here *made* me do. It must have been them who were controlling me, right? Bringing me here to pick you up, making me drive here without knowing why, like some kind of zombie. Did you know they did that to me? Do you think it was fun? There was nothing I could do about Dr. Viridian following me."

He sits slowly up in the seat, staring at me. "You know their names? They get you on their side? How much you tell them?"

"If I'm on anybody's side, I'm on your side, jerk! After all I've been through—like with your wonderful father, for instance—all you can do is accuse me of giving away somebody's secrets that I don't know anything about!"

"Oh, God, my father," he says and groans, sounding more like his old self. "Everything I saw, everything that's changed, everything that's going on—and I think I still dread dealing with him almost more than anything else. Funny . . ."

"But *what* have you seen, *what's* changed, *what's*

going on?" I glance over at him again, then back to the road. "You're older; I know that much. How . . . how long have you been away?"

"Thousands of years, Earth time, is what they said."

"Thousands of years?"

"We were traveling a lot—traveling really fast. Time dilation, you know . . . Only was a couple of years to us. So that's how much I aged."

"Yeah, but . . . How could you have been gone for thousands of years Earth time when you came back in only two days?"

"They brought me right back to this wonderful moment, of course," he says, as though it's stupid of me not to know that. His voice is a little clearer now, less garbled. "Time travel, Leo—otherwise you never would have seen me again. We were gone all that time, and then they just came back to right now. Why are they punishing me like this, making me come back here?" He laughs briefly, without humor, and shakes his head. "And of course they leave it up to *me* to figure out how to explain how I got older. Typical."

"Who's *they*?" I ask him.

He giggles again. "How much do you remember?" he asks me.

"Uh, now wait a minute," I say, suddenly angrier than before. I start slowing the car down. "What's so funny? Am I getting the feeling that you're not going to tell me what happened to you, what's really going on?

That you're just going to ask me what *I* remember? Because if that's what you're planning, you can get out of this car right now."

"I'll tell you, I'll tell you," he says in a placating voice. "But first I gotta find out what you remember, how much you know, what happened while I was gone. Only two days for you, right? If I tell you anything else before I hear your story, it might affect what you tell me."

What he says makes sense, but I'm still afraid he won't tell me everything once he's heard my story. Can I trust this new version of Tim? I try to come up with some threat to make sure he keeps his promise. "Okay. But if I tell you my story, and then you don't tell me yours, I'll go straight to The Others and I'll—"

"You *wouldn't!*" he says.

"Just keep your part of the bargain."

"I said I would!"

I speed up again. I tell him about blacking out the night he disappeared, about talking to his parents and the two cops and what his father and mother were like. I describe going to Dr. Viridian, the man who was chasing him just now, and being hypnotized and what I remembered then.

He snorts when he hears the green-men story.

"Just wait a minute!" I say hotly. I tell him why I doubted the story myself, and about being questioned by the police, and then going to the meeting tonight, and what was so peculiar about the stories everybody told. "So I figured all the stories were fake. That these hypnotists—I guess they're the ones you call The Others—changed our memories. First, so that none of us would know what really happened to us. And second, so that no one *else* would believe anything really happened to us at all. It seems like they don't want anybody to believe we were abducted by aliens."

"Pretty clever," he says, nodding. "And *really* clever of you to figure it out so fast, in only a couple of years, Leo; I've gotta hand it to you."

"It was only *two days* for me, remember? You just said so yourself."

"Oh, yeah. Only two days. That's right. So go on."

"And then when I left the meeting, something made me drive here and pick you up. I couldn't help it that the green van was following me. It was like I was being controlled by something."

"Squeeze your right earlobe," Tim says.

I do—and begin to panic again. "There's something in there, a hard little lump!" I say, my voice rising.

"They put it in you that night, when you were on the ship . . . so long ago."

"Yeah, but what *is* it?" I ask him, not liking having it there at all. "Something that makes it so they can control me?"

"Sometimes, to a certain extent, yeah, if absolutely necessary. Because of The Others. They don't like The Others."

"Who's they?" I ask him.

He doesn't say anything.

"Look, I told you my story. Now *you* have to tell me *something!*"

He doesn't say anything.

"Who's *they?*" I scream at him.

"The heads," Tim says.

When he says the word, I get a very ominous, surreal kind of feeling, like a flash of a memory from a bad dream. "The heads?" I say. "Is that who took us that night? Is that who you were with all this time?"

"What time is it here?" he asks me.

I sigh, because he's still avoiding telling me what happened to him, but I look at my watch. I can hardly believe it. "Oh, no, it's after two! I completely forgot about the time. My parents must be going nuts after what happened the other night and you disappearing and everything. We've got to get back."

"All right," Tim says, not sounding happy about it. "But could we go back to your house instead of mine? I'd like to go there first for a while, to kind of get ready to deal with my parents."

"Okay, I'll take you to my house on one condition: You tell me what happened to you," I say. "I'll start driving home now, and while I'm driving you talk—and talk fast."

And finally, while we're driving home, he tells me his story.

CHAPTER EIGHT

"THEY LOVED MY DRAWINGS!" TIM SAYS, HIS voice suddenly more animated.

"Huh?" I say, not understanding what he's talking about.

"The heads. They loved my drawings. That's why they kept me. They decided they wanted to make me into a really great artist."

"Uh, now wait a minute," I say very carefully. "You're telling me these aliens—these heads—kept you for all that time just because they liked your drawings?"

"Sure," he says brightly. "They love the whole idea of art—especially because I could do it with my own hands. The heads can't do anything like that, of course. And the bodies—well, the bodies can only do practical things, nothing artistic. Oh, sure, the pictures I was drawing all that time ago were really naive. I mean, creatures with superhero bodies and animal heads, you know?" He shakes his head and laughs. Then his voice grows excited again. "But they saw the potential in them, Leo! So they took me around, all over. I mean they gave me a real education. They showed me so many things to draw—*amazing* things." He squeezes his portfolio. "You want to see, Leo?" he says eagerly. "You're the only person I'm allowed to show them to. You could pull over somewhere and take a look at—"

"Sure, sure, later," I say, still completely mystified. If it weren't for the fact that he is so clearly older than he was two days ago, I wouldn't begin to believe any of this—and I still don't know if I trust him. "These heads. Are they the ones who abducted all those other people too? Is that what they're doing here, looking for artists?"

"Oh, they take other people too, for short times," he says in an offhand way. "But not because they're looking for artists. Don't be silly, Leo! It was just a lucky break that I happened to have my portfolio and—"

"But then why *do* they go around abducting people? Are they doing scientific experiments on us or trying to save the Earth or take over the Earth or—"

"The *Earth?* Oh, come *on!*" He flaps his hand at me as though what I'm saying is completely ridiculous. "They couldn't care less about the Earth. This planet is completely irrelevant. So anyway—the beginning was so long ago—once they got me to calm down, they told me my drawings were—"

"But if the Earth is completely irrelevant, then why *did* they abduct all those people? They must have done it for a reason."

He blinks, then shrugs. "I dunno. It's just something they do. I got the feeling that what they do with people

might have something to do with . . . The Others."
When he says "The Others," his voice changes, grows
hushed, and he stares off into the distance for a moment. Then he continues more slowly. "They never told
me exactly what they do with people, or why. It's some
kind of secret. I just know that The Others are their enemies, and dangerous. There's all these things they
don't want The Others to know. But so many wonderful things were happening that pretty soon I just
stopped asking about it. The first planet they took me
to was *amazing*, Leo! The creatures there!" He opens
his portfolio and starts quickly thumbing through it.

"Those people in the van that you were so afraid of.
You said they were The Others?"

"Uh-huh." He's still looking through his portfolio.

"But Dr. Viridian and Dr. Pierce are *people*, Tim.
The Others—the enemies of the heads—are they Earth
people, human beings?"

"No, no, no!" he says, as though I'm being stupid
again. "They're some other kind of alien."

"So how could you tell Dr. Viridian was one of The
Others if he looked just like a person?"

"Because they told me The Others might try to get
me, so I figured it was them. The Others are shape
changers—they can disguise themselves. It's not that interesting, Leo, and I'm not supposed to talk about it. I
wish I could see better, so I could find that drawing!"

In a way, it's typical: Tim has always been obsessed
with his artwork—and himself. But it's also odd that

when I first picked him up he was so afraid of Dr. Viridian and whoever else was in the van, and now that we're temporarily away from them, he dismisses them; he doesn't want to talk about them. Has he been brainwashed or something? Whatever the reason, I'm having trouble learning anything from him that might help us—such as how much danger we're really in.

"Tim, just forget about your drawings for a minute. It's too dark to see them anyway. Can you concentrate on what I'm saying? Tim! This is important."

He sighs. But he closes the portfolio and turns and looks at me. "Yeah?" he says.

"Don't you remember what I told you, about what happened while you were gone? The ones you say are The Others hypnotized the people who were abducted by the heads. The Others took their memories. They might know a lot more than the heads realize. Do you understand what I'm saying?"

He nods. "Sure. I haven't forgotten English, Leo."

His insouciance is more frightening than it would be if he were still terrified, simply because it's so irrational. He really *must* be brainwashed. "Look. If the heads are telling you the truth, don't you think they'd want to know what The Others found out?" I ask him, trying to be logical. "Like, what their enemies know about them? Not to mention *we're* not safe from The Others. They know my name. They know what you look like. That broken-down van won't stop them for very long. How are we going to hide from them? If this is true, why aren't you thinking about that? Aren't you afraid of what they'll do to us if they catch us—especially to you, because you were with the heads for so long?"

"Sure I am," he says.

I groan in frustration. "I mean, why did the heads just drop you back here, right in the middle of their enemies? Are they really going to protect you—and me? Is this part of some kind of plan, or what?"

"I already told you, Leo. I don't know very much about those things. That was all a secret from me."

"Did the heads make the green van stop?"

"They must have!" he says impatiently. "Look, all I know about that stuff is that The Others are dangerous. And I'm trying to tell you what I *do* know, the amazing things I *did* see. And you just keep worrying about The Others. Why worry about them *now?* They're not following us." He turns and looks out the back window and gestures. "See? There are no other cars on the road."

It's like he's a crazy person. He's not reacting to the situation he's describing. "Yeah, but they *will* be following us, Tim." I'm trying to be patient. "And what are we going to do when they catch up with us?"

We're on a different road now, closer to home. "Look, there's an all-night gas station," Tim says. "We'll be able to see my drawings under the lights there. Don't you want to look at just a few?"

I want to get home because of my parents and also because we might be a little safer there. Still, I *am* curious about his drawings. And once we get home, if we make it home, and have to deal with our parents—especially Tim's father—we won't have a chance to sit around looking at Tim's drawings. "Five minutes," I say and pull into the gas station.

"Of course the colors will look all wrong here, because of the bad lighting," he says. "But you should be able to get some idea."

When I see the first drawing, my heart sinks. Tim really *is* crazy; it's just a lot of scribbles.

But I keep looking. And as I do, the pictures begin to emerge—pictures that are all the more realistic and three-dimensional because they *do* consist of so many complex lines and cross-hatchings. I see several views of a rough-hewn city; all the buildings are carved out of translucent gems of various colors. It is a mountainous, vertical city designed for creatures who can fly: There are entrances to the buildings at all levels and no stairways or ramps or elevators. The bodies of the birdlike creatures flocking among the buildings are very small in relation to their wings, but their bald heads are quite large.

Their faces are streaked with blood. They are all eating what look like living humanoid creatures and dropping gobs of flesh to the ground. The countryside around the city is barren and arid, and the air is filled with smoke.

Tim was right about one thing, anyway: His drawings have really improved. They're hypnotic; the strange technique draws you in, so that it's hard to look away from them. "These are amazing, Tim. No kidding," I tell him. "Like—more than professional. Did you really draw these yourself?"

"Of course I did!" he snaps at me. "I can show you. I can draw one right now. I'll just get out a pencil and—"

"Okay, okay. You can do that later. What's this thing?"

"The harness other creatures wear so they can get around in that city." It's a metallic contraption reminiscent of armor, except that it has a very large balloon on it. "The Gratekteks have them for visitors who can't fly—they can adjust them to fit almost anything."

"Too bad you didn't have a camera. I mean so you could document that you really saw this and didn't just make it up," I say.

"Yeah, I wanted photos," Tim says. "And of course all the more advanced civilizations had cameras. But the heads wouldn't let me touch them. They wanted me to draw everything so I'd learn this style. Look at these. I have to show them to you in the right order so you'll get a sense of the scale."

He shows me a picture of a jungle. It could almost be a jungle on Earth, trees with long, bare trunks and dense foliage at the top creating a canopy. "See this tree here?" he asks me. "The one that's losing all the leaves?" I nod. "Okay. This next picture shows an enlargement of the bottom third of that tree. See the kind of weblike thread things here at the very, very bottom in the corner? I had to use a magnifier to draw them."

He shows me a series of pictures of the same scene, each one an enlargement of the one before. When I see the last one, I make a sound of amazement. The threads are not a spiderweb. They are the tracks of an amusement park ride, sort of like a roller coaster, with bulletlike vehicles on them. All the foliage around them is withered.

"The creatures who ride in these things are so *tiny* compared to the trees," I murmur. "To them, the trees must be like . . . like . . ."

"Gods," Tim says. "Gods that they kill. The exhaust from their vehicles does it."

There's something gruesome about the idea of these tiny creatures killing these huge trees just for their own amusement. And yet I want to keep looking. I pull my eyes away from the picture—it's an effort—and check my watch. "It's after three. We gotta go now."

"You have to look at this next drawing," he argues. "You haven't even seen any of the really special ones yet."

I make myself start the engine and drive out of the gas station. "I know you're not looking forward to see-ing your parents," I say. "But we have to do it some-time, and the later we are, the worse it's going to be."

For the next half hour, Tim tells me about traveling around the universe. "Of course the heads' ship goes faster than light—FTL travel for real! That's why thou-sands of years was only a couple of years to us. FTL travel has something to do with going through these wormholes in space."

"I still don't remember anything about what the heads were like or their ship or anything else at all," I say, feeling cheated—and still doubtful.

"The heads were pretty gross at first, but you got used to that. They're always joking around and laughing. They like to eat these worms that make them drunk. That's about the only physical thing they can do. The bodies are completely separate and do everything except think. And the ship is like nothing you would imagine. I mean it's a whole kind of muddy ecosystem, because they spend so much time there."

"You'd think my memory of it would come back, now that you're actually *telling* me," I say, jealous of him. "I almost wish the heads had brought me along too."

"Who knows, they may decide to let you come back to the ship again," Tim says.

"I said I *almost* wish it. Don't give them any ideas," I say quickly. His pictures distracted me for a while, but now I'm beginning to wonder how much of what Tim saw is real. He got a lot older in two days; there's no denying that. But did he *really* see all these planets, or did the heads just make him *think* he did? Obviously they have some kind of control over his mind—otherwise, he wouldn't be so frightened of The Others one minute and so blasé about them the next.

I keep checking the rearview mirror for the green van. I'm very relieved that there's no green van waiting for us when we reach my house. I'm almost happy to see the police car and that all the lights are on; we may be safe here for a while.

Tim balks when he sees his father's car is here too. "Why are the heads punishing me? Why did they have to bring me back here?" he moans.

I wish I knew. "Come on, Tim. You can't avoid it," I tell him. We start up the walk.

How is Tim going to explain what happened to him? The whole thing still baffles me. Tim's story really does not make much sense. Even if what he's saying is true, there are still a lot of unanswered questions. Why is Tim the only abducted person who remembers the heads and their ship? Did they really take him to all those worlds just to make him a great artist—or did they have some other secret motivation? And, most puzzling of all, why did they send him back into the midst of their enemies—these enemies that he is sometimes afraid of and sometimes *not* afraid of—with all these memories and drawings their enemies desperately want?

The answer hits me as we reach the door. I panic again, almost wishing Tim hadn't come back, wanting to stay as far away from him as possible now.

The Others want Tim and his drawings. Tim is what will bring them out of hiding; he is what will force them to reveal themselves more and more in their continued efforts to get him.

Tim is bait.

CHAPTER NINE

MOM AND DAD RUSH TOWARD ME AS SOON AS
we step inside. Tim's father and the two cops jump to
their feet and stare at us.

"What happened to you? Are you okay? Where were
you? Why didn't you call us?" Mom and Dad are saying.

"Everything's okay. Look—I found Tim!"

Now Mom and Dad turn and stare at him too. For a
long time, nobody says anything.

Captain Kroll breaks the silence. "Kind of an old picture of him you gave us," he says to Tim's father. "Would
have been easier to try to find him if you'd given us an up-
to-date one."

Mom backs to a chair and drops into it, her eyes
still on Tim. "My God," Dad murmurs. "What on
Earth?"

Tim just stands there holding his portfolio, his eyes
downcast, as if he's afraid to look at his father.

Now the cops seem confused, looking around at everybody. "What's the matter?" Captain Kroll says. "What's
going on here?"

"Yeah, I'd like to know that too," Tim's father says,

taking a step closer to us and narrowing his eyes. "What are you trying to pull *now*, Leo?"

Tim still isn't saying anything. He's leaving it all up to me. I feel like kicking him. "Uh . . . I know it's kind of hard to take in," I say to his father. "I was upset when I first saw him too. But now maybe you'll believe us about the aliens."

"I don't know what you're talking about," Tim's father says.

I turn to Captain Kroll. "That wasn't an old picture he gave you. The reason everybody's acting like this is that, well . . . Tim's a couple years older now than he was when they took him away the other night."

"What?" the cops both say at the same time.

"I wouldn't . . . I don't . . . But I can *see* it! No doubt about it," Dad says, shaking his head. "What on Earth *happened* to you, Tim?"

"Uh-huh, I should have expected that's what they'd do," Tim's father says, sounding disgusted. He turns to the cops and gestures at Dad. "Of course they're playing along with it too, to try to get their kid off the hook. But it's not going to work. This impostor he's dug up somewhere is not my son."

Tim still just stands there silently.

"Oh, come on!" I say to his father. "Okay, he's taller; he's lost a lot of weight. I know it's hard to believe. But try to stretch your mind a little. He's obviously the same person. Anybody can see that. Ask him something personal, some family thing. Ask him something nobody but Tim would—"

"This is ridiculous. I'm getting out of here," Tim's father says. He starts for the door, where we're still standing, then swings back to the cops. "Don't let up on the search," he orders them, then starts toward the door again.

"Please, Dad," Tim finally says, his voice quiet and calm. "Don't make everything worse; don't be embarrassing. For once in your life, could you please just try not to be so totally . . . rigid and superior."

Tim's father ignores him—he's shorter than Tim now—and instead marches up to me and glares into my face. "What did you think I'd do, let this stranger come and live in my house? You're not just criminal; you're *sick!*"

"And you're beyond belief!" I tell him. "Are you blind or something? Everybody else knows he's Tim. Come on, just ask him something. What are you going to lose?"

"Get out of my way and let me—"

"Mr. Coleman!" Captain Kroll interrupts him.

Tim's father turns around. "Yeah?" he says irritably.

"Everyone else *does* recognize him," Captain Kroll says, with an edge to his voice—he obviously hasn't enjoyed dealing with Tim's father. "Why *don't* you ask him something?"

"You too?" Tim's father says. "This is not my son."

"Your son was wearing a green-and-orange striped T-shirt and a pair of blue denim jeans and carrying a black portfolio on the night he was last seen," the second cop says, reading from his pad. "And so is this kid here."

"You know, you're right," Tim's father says, his eyes narrowing even more. He turns slowly back to Tim. "Those could very well be Tim's clothes this person is wearing. And you can see they don't fit him. And maybe there's some kind of scientific tests you can run on them, compare them to hairs or dandruff or whatever on Tim's other clothes or something, have a dog smell them or something, I don't know. But all you have to do is prove these are Tim's clothes on this impostor—and then you'll know for sure that Leo got rid of Tim somehow."

Now everybody except Tim shouts at each other for a while. Mom and Dad are defending me; Tim's father is accusing me; I'm telling Tim to come up with something, anything his family knows that nobody else knows; and Captain Kroll is trying to quiet us down. Finally he blows a painfully piercing whistle, and we all shut up and put our hands over our ears.

"Okay," Captain Kroll says to Tim. "If you really are who you say you are, you ought to be able to prove it, like Leo says. And nobody is moving or saying another word until you talk."

We wait silently. Tim looks at his father for a long time with an odd, speculative expression on his face. "Uh, I've been away for so long, my memory's kind of dim," he finally says, "but . . . remember the time we were on vacation in Florida, and we were at the beach, and your toupee blew off—the expensive one—and you had to chase it across the sand and all the people at the beach were laughing and pointing and telling their friends and—"

"No, I do not remember," Tim's father interrupts him, his voice unnaturally even. But we can all see his face getting redder and redder, and even as he is denying the story he can't keep himself from reaching up to be sure his hairpiece is in place.

"You know, I didn't even know you wore one," Captain Kroll says cheerfully. "That should make you feel better."

"I warn you, do not pay any attention to that impostor or you'll regret it," Tim's father threatens, though a lot of the bombast has gone out of his voice. "I'll check with your superior tomorrow to see how the search is going." He marches out of the house, slamming the door behind him.

"It's a true story," Tim says.

"I think he might have been more willing to admit your story was true if you'd come up with something that wasn't *quite* so embarrassing," Mom says. At the same time it's clear that she—and everybody else in the room —really enjoyed seeing Tim's father humiliated.

"Well, back to business," Captain Kroll says. He addresses Mom and Dad and me. "The three of you are saying this really is Tim—even though Mr. Coleman denies it?"

"It's Tim," I say.

"Well, he looks like Tim might look in two years—if he lost weight," Dad puts in. Mom agrees.

"So why are you so sure, Leo?" Captain Kroll asks me. "This stuff about getting two years older in two days is kind of hard to take, you know. Why are you so sure it's Tim and not just someone else who looks like him?"

"He acts like Tim. All he cares about is his drawings. Tim was always like that."

"Yes, but . . . did you make sure? Like what he knew about Mr. Coleman. Is there anything this guy knows that only Tim could know?"

I think back. I know he's Tim—I'm his best friend—but I realize we haven't discussed anything that had happened just between the two of us. Such as what we were talking about in the car before the heads abducted us.

"Do you remember much about the night when I was driving you to catch the bus to New York, before the heads came?" I ask him.

"Heads?" Mom says.

"What do you remember?" I ask Tim.

"That was such a long time ago, you know," he tells me. "Years and years."

"Yeah, but it was your last hour on Earth. Don't you remember anything?"

He sighs. "My last hour on Earth. And now I'm *back* here on Earth again," he says bitterly.

I want to ask him what exactly was so great about his trip that he didn't want to come home to his own planet, but now is not the time. "Like, what were you eating, for instance?" I prod him.

"Potato chips?" he asks me, his face brightening. "It

must have been potato chips. You got any here? Food, Earth food—that's what I miss more than anything else. It was about the *only* thing I missed, if you want to—"

"Yes, you were eating potato chips," I interrupt him. For some reason it bothers me hearing him complain about being returned to Earth. I turn to Captain Kroll. "He remembers eating potato chips when we were alone in the car, and he's right. Anyway, I already know it's him."

"*Do* you have any potato chips?" Tim asks Mom again.

"That's exactly the way Tim always sounded when he wanted something to eat," Mom says. "Yes, we do have potato chips. And while we're at it, how about a sandwich? Anybody else?"

Everybody declines except Tim.

"Okay," Mom says, "I remember your favorite combo, Tim. One pea—"

"Excuse me," Captain Kroll says. "Why don't you let him tell you what his favorite is."

Tim is almost panting now. "Peanut butter and salami and cheese with banana slices!" he bursts out.

"This is Tim. Couldn't be anybody else," Mom says. She goes over and kisses Tim on the cheek. "Welcome back, Tim," she says and pushes back her hair and walks into the kitchen. And I'm thinking how lucky I am to have parents like mine and not Tim's.

"Too bad Mr. Coleman doesn't agree about who you

are," Captain Kroll says, looking unhappy about it. "It would sure make things easier on us if he did."

"Compare his teeth. Test his DNA," I say. "Nobody can argue with data like that. Even that jerk—I mean, even his father would have to admit it then."

Soon the cops leave, telling us they will be in touch tomorrow. After Tim eats, Mom insists that we go to bed, saying we must be exhausted, and we can all talk in the morning. Tim and I go up to my room, where there are twin beds. But we're not exhausted; we're full of nervous energy. Sleep is impossible. I take a Polaroid of Tim, just for the heck of it. Then we talk quietly about Tim's adventures, and we look at more of his drawings—the "special" ones, he calls them.

Even in my worst nightmares, I have never seen anything like the first one he shows me.

CHAPTER TEN

"THIS IS A SPECIAL ONE," TIM SAYS. "WHAT do you think?"

I stare at it for a long time. This picture is even harder to make anything out of than the ones I looked at in the car, a mass of jagged lines in many subtly different colors. I know there must be something recognizable in here, but I can't seem to focus in on it.

"Try changing the distance from your eyes and the angle," Tim instructs me.

I move it back and forth; I shift the angle; I let my eyes blur a little. And then I see it. "Oh, no," I murmur. I feel very dizzy and have to shut my eyes. When I open them and look at the drawing again, my reaction is the same as if I've been slapped across the face. I feel it all over my body. It's painful, but at the same time I can't take my eyes away.

"Well? What do you think?" Tim presses me.

Partly it's the feeling of space that's so alarming. I'm staring directly down into a bottomless abyss; if I took one step I'd be falling down into it myself. The landscape around the abyss is eroded and defoliated, as though some great catastrophe has occurred here. Within the walls of the abyss are the awesome ruins of what was once a great civilization. It's so complex and detailed that you could go on looking at it for hours and still find more blackened, crumbling passageways, more bizarre alien artifacts strewn around. The streets that are not obstructed by collapsed buildings are clogged with rusting vehicles.

But most horrible of all are the creatures that are frolicking here. They are headless, toadlike things, with exposed veins and terrible, huge faces on their backs. They play in this wasteland with the same pleasure and excitement as monkeys swinging through a jungle. Somehow, Tim's drawing technique makes them more disgustingly realistic than any special effects.

"It's great, Tim. I've never seen anything like it. It's sensational. But why do all your drawings have to be so . . . *horrible?*"

He doesn't answer my question. "You really think it's sensational?" he asks me, basking in my praise.

"You didn't actually *see* this, did you?"

"It was a hologram broadcast. We saw lots of wonderful things on holograms."

I hand the drawing back to him, shaking my head. "I think you've changed more than physically, Tim. I mean, sure, you were always self-involved when it came to your artwork. But you were never bloodthirsty. You have any drawings at all that *don't* have something gruesome in them?"

"People *like* gruesome things," Tim says. "All intelligent creatures do."

"Yeah, but every once in a while, just for a break, your audience might want to see something that isn't just like a horror film."

He looks down shyly, leafing through his portfolio. "Well, I do have some different ones. But . . . they're kind of personal."

"What do you mean, *personal?* What are you hiding?"

He looks away, holding a picture in his hand that he seems reluctant to show me. "I . . . I mean . . ."

"Tim, you *can't* hide things from me. We're in a really tight situation, with these Others after us. You have to tell me everything or we won't make it." I think for a moment. "Those other drawings you showed me in the car—the city of flying creatures, the city under the tree. Did you really go to those places, or were those just holograms the heads showed you too?"

"Oh. They were holograms too."

"So how do you know any of these places are real and not just fantasy movies that the heads *told* you were real?"

Tim thrusts the picture in his hand at me, almost angrily. "They're real. I trust the heads. And I really *did* spend a lot of time on this planet." His voice softens. "I . . . I really know her."

My eyes seem to be learning the trick of interpreting the lines more easily. It's a drawing of a young woman. She seems almost human. She has no hair, and her face and limbs and body are thin and elongated. Even so, she's very beautiful. She's sitting on the ground, with her arms, like tree branches, stretched out behind her, supporting her. She's looking directly at the viewer. Aside from her strange beauty, the most striking thing about the picture is its luminous quality. The sky seems to be glowing directly behind her, so that she is surrounded by a kind of halo.

"You really knew her?" I ask him.

"I really *know* her!" he says fiercely. "And I'll be with her again; I'll go back to her, no matter what!" He pulls the drawing away from me and gazes down at it. His eyes are brimming with tears.

Now I feel shy. I don't know what to say. He seems to be in love with this alien girl. That's a big change too. Before he went away, he was too preoccupied with his artwork—and mainly too self-conscious about his weight—to get involved with girls.

"Who is she?" I finally ask him.

"Chaweewan," he says, his voice husky, continuing to stare down at her.

Now I know why he's so unhappy about being returned to Earth. "Where does she live?"

"A planet called Sawan. It means . . . it means *heaven* in their language," he manages to say, his voice choking up. He gulps and continues. "Before they took me there, I was upset about being abducted. I think they hoped this world, Sawan, would change my mind about what was happening to me. And they were right." He sniffs and wipes his nose. "Uh, it's smaller than the Earth and more primitive, because they're more cautious—you might say superstitious. They won't use any advanced technology or even anything as primitive as internal combustion engines. So they use animals to get around, instead of cars and jets. It's all rural. The people live on farms and are all pretty self-sufficient. They know that other creatures, like the heads, have more advanced technology, but they're not interested. They're kind of stupid in that way."

"Who says they're stupid? It sounds a lot better than the other planets you drew pictures of. In a way, this place . . . uh, Sawan . . . almost sounds better than the Earth."

"The heads think the Sawanese are dumb, running away from technology. But anyway, the Sawanese are physically pretty close to human beings, so the heads thought it might cheer me up to go there. It sure did." He sighs unhappily. "It was the best thing that ever happened to me. And she didn't care that I was fat."

"You were still fat then?"

"Uh-huh. It was one of the first places they took me. Sawan is smaller than Earth, so there's less gravity, and it was so easy for me to run, to jump. And I was still in the middle of my growth spurt then. That's why I got so tall— having my growth spurt on a planet with lower gravity. That's why I started looking a bit like her. She didn't mind when I was fat, but she . . . she likes me better like this. Every time I went back, it was more wonderful with her."

"You went there more than once?"

"Yeah, they took me back several times, to keep my spirits up." He pauses. "And then, tonight, the heads just suddenly dropped me off here—about as far away from Sawan as you can get."

"They didn't tell you they were going to bring you back here?" The heads—with their contempt for ecological thinking, and the ugly places they mostly took Tim to or showed him, and the way they didn't explain to him where they were taking him—are beginning to seem distinctly unpleasant to me.

"No, they didn't. They just suddenly said, 'Well, here we are. Your friend will pick you up. Watch out for The Others. Don't let them get your drawings.' That was it. And I went nuts. I refused to go. So they gave me one of their injections. That's why I was sort of out of it when you picked me up. That's why I wasn't very upset about what they did—until now." He clenches his fists. "They *will* take me back to her; they've *got* to!"

"Shhh!" I tell him. "My folks will know we're awake."

Then we just sit there for a while. Tim's being a little unrealistic, thinking he'll ever see his alien girlfriend again, but I don't tell him that, not wanting to make him more upset. Anyway, I'm more worried about other things he's told me. The more I think about his story, the more scared I am.

Finally I ask him, "Do you have any idea at all why the heads brought you back here at this particular time?"

He silently shakes his head, still blinking back tears.

"Well, I do. I don't trust the heads one bit, after what you've told me about them. This is a trap."

"I don't know what you're talking about," he says indifferently, looking down at the picture of Chaweewan again.

"The heads are using you, Tim. Don't you see that?"

Again he says, "I don't know what you're talking about."

"They gave you exciting adventures. They gave you the first girlfriend you've ever had. They got you to think they were good guys. But they didn't tell you anything about their real motives. And then they drop you back here, completely ignorant, in the middle of their enemies—their enemies who are always looking for information about the heads and who are dying to get their hands on you, because you were with the heads for so long. Don't you see what they're doing?"

He shakes his head, wiping his eyes, not the least bit alarmed by what I'm saying.

"Forget about Chaweewan for a minute. The heads are setting a trap for The Others. And they're using you as the bait."

"I don't know what you're talking about."

I want to scream. "It's obvious! You're a worm on a hook!"

He shrugs. "So they're using me as bait. They'll rescue me before The Others can hurt me."

I sigh. "How do you know that, Tim? They're putting you—not to mention me—in a dangerous position. And what they care about is getting The Others, not your safety."

"They wouldn't let The Others hurt me," Tim says, refusing to listen to reason. "And they'll take me back to Chaweewan too."

"You'll see," I tell him, feeling sorry for him but also irritated at his refusal to face facts.

My prediction comes true sooner than I expected. The moment after I speak, I hear the soft purr of engines and the delicate crunch of tires on the gravel driveway. My room is at the front of the house. I race to the window.

The light over the front door is on. I see the green van drive up, followed by two other cars. The cars are full of dark figures, who emerge quickly and silently and take their places around the house.

Chapter Eleven

"The Others!" I tell Tim, not whispering now. "They're surrounding the house!"

"Huh?" He looks up from the picture, finally a little startled. "How do you know?"

"It's the same green van that was following me when I picked you up. And other cars too. There's a lot of them, Tim. This must be what the heads have been waiting for—a lot of them all together in the same place."

Tim just sits there looking puzzled. I don't wait for him to take it all in. "Don't leave this room unless they try to get in here," I order him. I close and lock both windows.

I hurry out of the room. "Mom! Dad!" I yell. "Get up! This is an emergency! We're surrounded!"

I hear muffled expostulations from their room, but I don't wait. I pound down the stairs. I know the front and back doors are locked, but I check them just to make sure. Then I start on the downstairs windows. It might be pointless—The Others are aliens; they could have some way of getting in through locked doors and windows—but I don't know what else to do. I don't turn on the lights, because I don't want them to be able to see what's going on inside. All I can see outside are vague, dark shapes. They're clustered around the front windows. They seem to be just standing there.

"What's going on, Leo?" Dad demands angrily.

I turn from the window. Mom and Dad are in the middle of the dark living room. Behind them, Tim is coming slowly down the stairs, cradling his portfolio in his arms.

"Tim, what are you doing down here?" I'm furious. "I told you to stay upstairs. And you shouldn't have brought your drawings with you!"

"I . . . I can't go anywhere without my portfolio," he says, and I wonder if that might be a command from the heads, through the implant in his ear.

Before I have a chance to tell Tim to go back upstairs, Dad steps to the side and reaches for the light switch.

"Don't turn it on!" I tell him. "They'll be able to see us."

"Who's they?" Dad snaps at me. But he doesn't turn on the light.

"Come and look. There are three cars out in front, and the house is surrounded."

"Huh?" Mom and Dad hurry over to the window.

"See? See how many there are at the front windows?"

Mom backs away and turns to me. "Who are these people?"

"I never had a chance to tell you." I explain what I figured out at the meeting, about the doctors changing our memories. I tell them about being compelled to pick Tim up and that the same van was following me with Dr. Viridian in it and how he tried to get at Tim. "These creatures here, The Others, are the enemies of the heads—the heads are the ones who abducted Tim. The Others want to get Tim, because he was on the heads' ship for so long, he knows stuff about them. They also want Tim's drawings. And I think the heads are setting a trap. They sent Tim back so The Others would congregate, to try to catch Tim. And now— they're here."

The doorbell rings. Dad starts toward it.

"Dad, you can't open it!"

"Now look, Leo, we have to find out what these people want," he says, still moving, obviously not believing my story.

I jump in front of the door and spread my arms.

Dad points his finger at me. "Get out of my way, Leo!"

The doorbell rings again, and in the next instant someone is banging on the door. "Tim!" his father's voice says. "It's me, your father. I want to talk to you. Let me in!"

Dad's hand drops. "But . . . he didn't recognize him before." He just stands there.

"Tim," I say, my mouth dry. "Do you think maybe your dad could be one of them too?"

Tim is slowly shaking his head. "But how . . . how could he . . ."

"Maybe that's why he claimed you weren't his son," I slowly say. "Because he doesn't want the cops to know you came back. Because if they don't know you came back, then they won't notice if you . . . disappear again."

Tim doesn't say anything. He squeezes his portfolio against his chest, backing away from the door.

The banging on the door starts up again. "I want to talk to my son!" Tim's father yells.

"He's Tim's father," Mom says.

"Wait!" Before Mom and Dad can move, I desert my protective position at the door and rush to the phone. "We have to call the cops." I lift the receiver—and then slam it down again. "The phone's dead," I tell them. "Now do you believe me?"

"The phone's dead . . ." Mom says, sounding confused, as though the concept is beyond her.

"They cut the line so we can't call for help," I tell her.

"I want to talk to my son!" Tim's father shouts and bangs on the door again.

"At least they don't seem to be able to get in on their own," I say. I turn to Tim. "How much do you know about The Others? Is there anything else you haven't told me?"

"I just know they're the enemies of the heads. And they're shape changers. That's all they told me."

More banging on the door. "I'm sorry . . . for what I did before," Tim's father says. "I know it's really you, Tim. I just . . . couldn't accept how you've changed. But now I understand. Please let me in so we can talk."

"Am I hearing things?" Tim mumbles. "I didn't think 'I'm sorry' was part of his vocabulary." Tim moves closer to the door. "What do you want to talk about?" he shouts.

"We just want you to come home, where you belong. Your mother and I are so worried. Come on, let me in! I don't like standing out here screaming in the middle of the night."

"This is ridiculous. Of course he has to talk to Tim," Mom says, and before I can stop her, she dashes to the door and flings it open.

She screams. In a rush, the shape-changing Others flow through the door on either side of Tim's father— who still looks like Tim's father and remains standing in the doorway. The formless gray shadows swarm around Tim in a kind of whirling vortex. Mom keeps screaming. Dad and I try to pull Tim back, but we can't touch him. The Others *look* like you could reach right through them, but they are not like clouds; they are solid, a dense wall around Tim. They pull Tim—with his portfolio—out into the night. His father, legs spread, standing in the doorway, throws back his head and laughs and then slams the door shut. In a split second, the cars are pulling out of the driveway.

"Dad, quick! The car keys! We have to follow them."

"Not you, Leo," Dad says, his voice implacable. "You're too vulnerable—because of what happened to you before. I'll go myself." He dashes up the stairs to get dressed.

Mom sits huddled in a chair, and I pace; neither of us turns on a light or speaks. I feel scared and helpless. But Dad is right. There's an implant in my ear. If I'm out there in a car, who knows what the heads might make me do?

In a few minutes, Dad rushes down the stairs.

"It's too late to follow them now," I tell him.

"I'm going to the cops. They need to know what happened," he says. He hugs Mom and tells her everything will be fine. He orders me not to leave the house, to stay and take care of Mom—and not to let anybody in, even if I think I know who it is, until he comes back. And then he's gone. I hurry to lock the door. We hear the car drive away fast.

Mom sighs. "We should both try to get some rest," she says and pushes herself unsteadily out of the chair.

I can't imagine sleeping. But I take Mom's arm and go with her up the stairs.

"I'm sorry I opened the door, Leo," Mom says.

"Well, things might still turn out okay, maybe," I tell her.

But I don't believe what I'm saying. They have Tim

and his drawings. How could it be any worse? I push open the door of my room.

And there, on the bed, are the drawings.

My knees go weak with relief. I can hardly believe Tim had the wits to do this. But somehow he was thinking clearly. He saw the possibility that The Others might take him. And so he brought his portfolio—and left the drawings here.

There must be information or a message in the drawings that the heads don't want The Others to see. I'm very eager to look at them more carefully—even though most of them are so gruesome—to see if I can find the message myself. But I stifle the impulse. The most important thing is to hide them. I rummage around in my closet and find an ancient, tattered back-pack and carefully put the drawings inside it. I look around the room, considering. Then I bury the back-pack underneath the mess of old shoes and camping equipment and tennis rackets at the bottom of my closet, making sure the backpack is way in the back. I turn out the light and lie down on the bed with all my clothes on.

I know I won't be able to sleep. What's happening to Tim? Are they hypnotizing him to unearth the memo-ries the heads suppressed? Are they giving him drugs to make him talk? Are they doing something *worse* to make him talk? And where are they? I can't believe they just went to Tim's house; that would be too obvious. They must have a more secret hiding place, somewhere the heads can't locate them, even with Tim's implant. And anyway, Tim didn't say the implant was a tracking device; he just said they could control you with it sometimes.

And why didn't the heads do something while The Others were here, before Mom let them into the house? *That's* when I would have expected them to make their move. I'm more baffled than ever by the motivation of the heads. What are they really up to? It's all so confusing. My eyes begin to close.

I'm awakened by a slight vibration, so subtle it could have been a part of a dream. At first I think it's morning, because the room is full of light.

And then I see that the light is not coming through the windows, which are still dark. It's coming from some impossible place above the ceiling of my room. And it's not daylight. It's an intense amber beam focused directly on my bed. I feel like I'm going crazy. I try to scream, but I have no voice.

I rise into the air.

Chapter Twelve

THE AMBER LIGHT IS LIFTING ME UP TOWARD the ceiling of my room. My heart is racing wildly; sweat is breaking out all over me. But I can't scream; I can't move; I'm immobilized, which only makes it all more terrifying.

I'm moving faster; the ceiling is getting closer; I'm going to crash into it. But I don't. I float right through the ceiling, into the attic, and then up through the roof of the house.

This is impossible; it can't be happening. Yet somehow I know with absolute certainty that it *is* happening; it's not a dream; it's real.

Now I can see the peaked roof of the house getting smaller as I rise more and more swiftly into the air. I can see other houses and trees and roads, the landscape spreading out below me as I'm lifted higher and higher. It's almost dawn; the light is golden on the horizon.

And now I can see what's above me too—the amber lights of the small, round craft hovering high in the air directly over our house. And then I am inside it.

Suddenly I know I've been here before. In this place

my memory rushes back. It's all familiar: the rotten smell; the spongelike seat I'm lowered into; the rubber cable around my waist; the sudden, stomach-sinking rush as the vehicle zooms high into the stratosphere. And the creatures. It's too dark to see them clearly, yet I know what they look like: tall and thin, with arms like tentacles and heads the size of tennis balls with an eye on either side and a mouth that goes all the way around. But even though it is familiar, I am no less horrified. This is what I dreaded would happen again! I'd be screaming and thrashing if I had the power to utter sounds or to move.

But I'm still immobilized. And I remain immobilized when we lock into the mother ship and the round aperture opens. Paralyzed, I float down the corridor, surrounded by the tall ones. I enter the large room, full of the gently swaying trees. They seem taller and fuller this time, as if they have grown since I was last here. There are garments hanging up to dry and soiled garments and cans and other objects lying haphazardly around on the dirty floor. And I can see more this time. Above the trees, in the center of the domed ceiling, there is something like a huge, delicately faceted stained-glass window with an amber glow. As nightmarish as this is, I am also aware that the window is very beautiful. Is that where Tim saw the gruesome holograms?

The heads are waiting, as repulsive as ever with their loose folds of skin; their many bug eyes; their wet, drooping mouths, into which they are constantly sliding the wriggling creatures they seem to be addicted to. They do not say anything until I am strapped into the stained reclining chair, and my blood has been taken, and I have then been injected with the drug that makes me a little calmer.

Again, they speak directly into my brain. *Welcome back, Leo. We are sorry about Tim. But we are afraid it could not be—*

And then something changes. The voice stops briefly, replaced by a feeling of confusion. When the voice comes back, there is a frozen quality to it.

We are not happy with what you did. We can see in your mind what happened. You and Tim made a terrible mistake.

I can talk now, maybe because of the injection. "How could we know what's a mistake and what's not a mistake if you never told us what to do? I did everything I could to protect Tim."

So you say, Leo. But The Others do not have the drawings. The Others were supposed to get the drawings.

I can hardly believe what I'm hearing. "You *wanted* The Others to get the drawings? Then why did you tell Tim to keep the drawings *away* from The Others? Why did you stop The Others from getting the drawings when I picked Tim up?"

We don't want to hear your excuses, Leo. We are very disappointed in you.

Horrible as it was the first time I was here, this time

is a lot worse. Before, they were genial and pleasant. Now they are angry. And what they are angry about makes no sense to me at all. Why are they saying they *want* The Others to have the drawings? I think of the violent and catastrophic scenes they showed Tim, their supposed drawing lessons. What kind of bloodthirsty creatures are they? What are they really doing? I am completely powerless, under their control. Sweat is pouring down my forehead, stinging my eyes, and I can do nothing to wipe it away.

"But why didn't you get The Others when you had the chance and so many of them were outside my house? Did you let them take Tim on purpose, because you wanted them to get the drawings?"

They do not respond. They are conferring together, out of my range, their antennae swaying as they look at one another, their eyes rolling.

Then they turn and look at me. *We are trying to decide whether or not to punish you,* they inform me.

The blood in my veins turns to ice water. "Punish me? But how was I supposed to know what to do if you never told me, if you made me forget I was ever here? And if there was something you wanted us to do, why did you tell Tim the opposite?"

We didn't tell Tim about the situation because he is a dreamer, an artist. Strategy and war are not his talents; he is useless to us in that realm. But you are a person of action, Leo. We expected more of you.

"But—"

Above me the trees are swaying and bending more deeply. Behind them, three-dimensional images flow across the screen—ruined cities, the streets clogged with abandoned vehicles; dried-up oceans and barren landscapes, all wreathed in black, toxic clouds. What does it mean? Is it a threat?

Listen. We will not punish you—not now, anyway. Because this is what you are going to do. You will bring the drawings to Tim's father's office. You will leave an urgent message for him there, to come and pick up the drawings. We do not know where The Others are hiding. But we know his father will check back with his office regularly. And then The Others will get the drawings. You will do this whether you want to or not. Because of the implant.

Terrified as I am, I am so baffled and upset that I can't keep from protesting. "But this is crazy! If you want us to do something, why not just tell us why? Tell us what your plan really is! Then maybe we'll do the right thing."

We do not need to tell you, because the implant will make you do it. You are human; humans are dangerous, ruled by greed and emotion. That is why it is better that you do not know any more than necessary.

A planet rotates on the screen above me, a pockmarked planet devoid of all life—though the smoking ruins make it clear that not long ago there was a great civilization here. The heads blast me with a message more powerful than anything they have said before. *Of utmost importance: No other humans must see those drawings. Only The Others must see them. You will wait at Tim's father's office until he comes to get them and give them to him yourself—and you will make it clear that you are doing this of your own volition, not because of us. The implant is your helper. And remember—if any other humans see the drawings, the result will be a catastrophe beyond your imagination.*

I notice that the bodies have just taken my blood again, but that isn't my main concern. I have to find out more. But before I have the chance even to ask a question, the cables have loosened; I'm rising into the air again. I'm shouting at them like crazy, begging them to explain, to tell me what is really going on, asking them why they let The Others get Tim. They have turned away, ignoring me. I am propelled back to the smaller ship, accompanied by the tall ones. We detach from the mother ship and descend. The beam of amber light takes me from the small ship back down through the roof of the house and deposits me on my bed.

Morning light is streaming through the windows. For a moment I just lie there, disoriented, full of panic like I have never felt before. I want to stay in bed, to let myself recover, to try to stop panicking and figure out what might really be going on.

But the heads don't give me a chance. Before I really know what I'm doing, I am up; I am opening my closet door; I am rummaging through the mess on the floor and unearthing the backpack with the drawings.

I look out the window. The car is there; Dad has returned. I know Mom keeps her car keys in her handbag, which is downstairs. I move quietly, not wanting to wake them up, because if I do they will stop me.

I don't know where Tim's father's office is, but that doesn't matter. The heads will guide me there—the same way they guided me to the spot where I picked up Tim.

But even though they are controlling part of me, I am still conscious, like I was when I picked up Tim. The difference is that this time I know exactly what is happening to me.

And because now I *do* know what is happening to me, my conscious brain is determined—more than anything else in the world—to resist.

Chapter Thirteen

I TRY TO GO AS SLOWLY AS POSSIBLE, TO GIVE myself time to think, resisting the implant's command to hurry downstairs, get in the car, and drive downtown. It's a terrible struggle, like trying to stay calm and not to run when all the adrenaline in your body is telling you to get away as fast as possible. And yet—*because* I know the implant is doing this to me—I am able to move at a crawl. I push open the door of my room; I creep toward the stairway.

My mind is going very fast. I know for sure now that I can't trust the heads. They lie. They told Tim they didn't want The Others to see the drawings, when in fact that is exactly what they *do* want. That must be why they gave Tim the command never to go anywhere without his portfolio: They were hoping The Others would capture him, so that they would get the drawings. Like the Earth, Tim is irrelevant to them.

The implant is pushing me toward the stairs. But I need more time. With a tremendous effort, panting, I turn toward the bathroom door. "You can't stop me from going to the *bathroom*," I whisper. I know the heads can't hear me, but possibly the implant under-stands a little about human physiology. As I move to-ward the bathroom, the pressure to go down the stairs lessens slightly. I step inside and close the door.

So if they want The Others to have the drawings, why did they stop the green van, when Dr. Viridian could easily have gotten Tim and the drawings then, as soon as I picked Tim up? I know there's an explanation, and it has to do with something they said to me just now, when I was on their ship.

I move toward the medicine cabinet. I know that's where the solution is to my immediate predicament—the compulsion I'm fighting to drive to Tim's father's office.

Then I remember what the heads said on the ship. When I give the drawings to Tim's father, they want me to make sure he thinks it is my own idea and not a command from the heads. The heads want The Others to think they *don't* want them to have the drawings. That's why they said that to Tim. And that's why they saved us from the green van—so that The Others would believe the drawings were being kept from them, which would make them want them even more. After all, if The Others knew the heads *wanted* them to have the drawings, then they would be wary of them; they would probably have nothing to do with them.

I open the medicine cabinet. Dad's razor blades are on the bottom shelf.

I see now with absolute clarity that I must not do what the heads are commanding me to do. I know this because of the way the heads lie, the way they don't explain, and the way they threaten. They made Tim draw these sadistic pictures—pictures with some kind of secret message in them. They have contempt for human beings and for our planet. They want The Others to get the drawings, and they want no other human beings to see them.

I must do exactly the opposite of what they want: keep the drawings away from The Others and show the drawings to as many human beings as possible. I must refuse to be controlled by the heads' implant.

But now the implant is getting impatient; I've been in the bathroom long enough. The compulsion to hurry down the stairs and drive away is strengthening, getting more and more difficult to fight. In another few seconds, I know I won't be able to resist it any longer.

The need to remove the heads' repellent artifact from my body is a feeling as strong as the need to take my next breath.

Even as I am fighting the overpowering urge to get out of here, I reach for an unused razor blade—the newer it is, the sharper it will be. I remove the paper wrapping. Watching myself in the mirror, I grasp my right earlobe with my left thumb and finger, feeling the implant there. I pull it down as far as I can. Holding the razor blade in my right hand, I begin slicing through my earlobe just above the implant.

The command of the implant is so strong that my upper body is leaning toward the bathroom door, as though being pulled by a magnet, even while I am fighting to keep my feet planted firmly in place in front of the mirror.

The razor slides into the skin. A line of bright blood appears. I pull the razor deeper. The blood begins to drip out, making red drops on the white porcelain sink. It begins to trickle, then to flow, as the razor moves in deeper.

It also begins to hurt like crazy. I try to ignore the pain and keep the razor moving. I picture the heads, how disgusting they are, how much I don't want this thing of theirs inside my flesh. But the implant is still pulling me toward the door, and the pain is intense. I can't help it; I whimper, I moan, I make louder noises. It doesn't matter if Mom and Dad hear me; in fact, I *want* them to see this implant, just in case they have any further doubts about the reality of what is going on.

I scream, and with one last pull of the razor I slice off the bottom part of my earlobe.

The compulsion to drive from the house instantly vanishes. With my left hand I deposit my earlobe on the edge of the sink. I quickly squeeze the cut skin together to try to stop the blood gushing out all over the place and with my other hand open the medicine cabinet and reach frantically for the Band-Aids.

Mom and Dad come bursting into the room. I don't look at them; I'm trying to get a Band-Aid to stick to my mutilated ear. I hear Mom scream, and then she is beside me, pulling gauze and tape out of the cabinet, cleaning and bandaging my ear.

"What did you *do?*" Dad is shouting at me. "Have you gone out of your mind?"

"I . . . I cut out the implant," I say, feeling a little faint now.

"Implant? What are you talking about?"

"The heads . . . put it in, so they could control me. But I won't let them. So . . . I had to cut it out."

Then we don't say anything, while Mom finishes with my ear. "Come on, Leo. Sit down," she urges me when it's all gauzed and bandaged and pulls me toward the toilet seat.

I pluck the severed earlobe from the sink as I go. I slump down on the toilet. I feel steadier sitting down.

"Okay, what's this all about?" Dad says. They are both very pale as they stare down at me, their faces still creased from sleep.

I hold out the earlobe. "Feel this," I say.

They both shrink away. "Do you know what you're doing, Leo?" Dad says.

They think I'm going crazy. "Okay, if you won't feel it, then I'll show it to you," I say. I am still holding the razor blade and the earlobe. I start cutting into the earlobe to try to expose the implant.

But of course this only makes them more convinced I've gone insane. Mom reaches for my hands. "Leo, stop that, please!" she begs me. "It's horrible."

"It's the only way I can prove to you what I did," I say, slicing delicately at the earlobe with the razor blade. "The heads put something in here, something that could control me. I had to get it out, so they can't command me to do what they want anymore." Finally I get a hole in the edge of the earlobe and squeeze, and something slides out into my palm.

It's a cylinder about a quarter of an inch long, made out of what looks like bright yellow plastic, with a sharp metal point extending from each end. I hold it up. "See this? *This* was what was inside my earlobe. You think this is natural? I had to get it out. It was going to make me give Tim's drawings to The Others."

Neither of them wants to touch it. But their expressions change as they stare down at it. They look back at my face, their eyes widening. "You saw me take this out of my ear. It's an alien device that was implanted there. They used it to control me. Now do you understand why I had to take it out? I *couldn't* let those creatures be in control of me!"

"Last night . . . and now this," Mom says, her face ashen. She sinks down onto the edge of the bathtub as though her legs won't support her.

Dad is staring at the implant again. Then he gulps and looks away. "This is some kind of nightmare," he says. "It's beyond belief. What can we do?"

"I've got a plan," I say. "I'll need the car."

"Where will you go?" Mom asks fearfully.

"First I go to the cops. And after that I go to Channel Three."

Chapter Fourteen

We decide it will be best if Mom comes with me. Dad will take care of getting the phone line repaired—he'll have to call the phone company from next door.

Before we leave the house, I find out from Dad what happened when he went to the cops last night. They were skeptical about The Others taking Tim and especially skeptical about Tim's father being one of them. But they did go to Tim's house. Tim's parents were both there, his mother bland and emotionless, his father angry at being awakened when there was no news of their son. Tim's father denied again that the boy I found was Tim. He accused Dad of hallucinating when he told him about the gray shapes and him being with them. "So what if that strange boy disappeared?" Tim's father said. "It's no concern of ours." And that was the end of it, last night.

But now I have the implant to show the cops.

I'm glad Mom is with me at the police station—even though they were skeptical of what Dad said last night, they always take adults more seriously than they do kids. Mom verifies that the yellow object came out of my earlobe, that no doctor ever put it in there, and that in fact there was no scar to indicate the heads had implanted it—even though she saw me pull it out. Their technology is very advanced.

Captain Kroll doesn't spend a lot of time questioning the authenticity of the implant. He puts it in an envelope and says it will be sent to the lab for analysis.

"Please let us know as soon as you find out anything about it—what it's made of, what's inside it, anything," I say. "It's urgent. The Others have Tim. Who knows what they're doing to him? We've got to find him as soon as possible."

"Sure, sure," Kroll says, sighing and shaking his head.

"And . . . you do have somebody following Tim's father, right?" I ask him. "It's really important."

"No, we don't," he says shortly. His good nature seems to be wearing thin.

It's an effort to control my impatience. "But he knows where Tim is," I say, trying to keep my voice steady. "Following him is the way to find Tim before it's too late."

"We have no reason to believe he knows where his son is. We have no reason to believe the boy who . . . disappeared last night really is Tim."

"But all three of us saw The Others . . . and Tim's father . . ." My voice fades. It *does* sound crazy, here in the police station. I'm not stupid enough to tell him about being abducted myself again last night.

"Yes?" he says, eyeing me steadily.

"But now you have the implant," I say. "And if you find out anything about it that seems to show it doesn't come from the Earth, then you'll *have* to believe us. When you find that out, *then* will you start following Tim's father?"

"We'll see," he says. The phone on his desk rings. "I'm kind of busy," he says.

"Could you please hurry? Tim's in danger," I urge him. We leave as he is answering the phone.

"A washout," I say as we walk to the car. "And I thought he was on our side. Doesn't he realize how much danger Tim is in?"

"It's hard to believe, Leo," Mom says. "I'm still shaken up by it, but for somebody who didn't actually *see* it, it's different."

"Well, they'll see when they analyze that implant," I say, wondering if I'm right. "I hope it won't be too late to save Tim."

"I'm afraid they won't let you past the reception desk at Channel Three," she says when we get into the car.

"They've got to," I say.

Channel Three is the local TV station. Tim's disappearance has been on the news. I'm hoping Tim's case—and the drawings—might get somebody in the newsroom to listen to me. After all, it's a story, and from what I can tell, TV stations are always looking for stories.

I've never been inside the building before. Through the glass doors is a receptionist at a desk, who smiles perfunctorily through her mask of makeup, politely not reacting to my bandaged ear. No doubt her major function is to keep people like us from bothering anybody else who works at the station.

I'm nervous; I know I have to move as fast as possible because of what might be happening to Tim. But I also know I have to act calm and rational, or else nobody will listen to me.

"We need to talk to somebody in the newsroom," I say to the receptionist. "It's important. It's about the Tim Coleman case—the boy who disappeared three days ago. I was with him when he disappeared. And now we have some special information about him."

She hesitates. "Don't you think the police would be the people to talk to about that?" she says pleasantly.

"Yes, we're working with Captain Kroll; we just came from there," I explain. "And we have some very newsworthy information. Just take a look at this. Maybe you'll see what I mean."

I have the drawing all ready just inside my backpack—the very special drawing that made me feel dizzy and shocked when Tim showed it to me in my room. I hand it to the receptionist. "You've got to move it back and forth, tilt it a little to get the right angle. Then it will come into focus."

Now she glances a little uncertainly at my ear. But she takes the drawing; she moves it forward and back in front of her eyes. She doesn't really seem to have a lot to keep her busy on this job.

I can tell when the picture comes into focus, because suddenly she goes pale under her makeup. She peers forward, frowning. She stares at it for what seems like a full minute. Finally she hands it back to me, looking confused. "Where did you get this?" she asks me. "What does it have to do with the missing boy?"

"He was abducted by aliens. He drew these pictures while he was with them. They brought him back last night—two years older. And then the other aliens took him away again."

"Aliens?" she says, looking back and forth between us. If it weren't for the drawing, she'd probably have us thrown out right now. And she still might do it anyway.

I nudge Mom's foot with my own. "I'm Lenore Kasden. This is my son, Leo," Mom says. "My husband and I saw the aliens too."

"Aliens?" the receptionist says again. But I can tell by the way she looks at Mom that she doesn't think she's crazy. "Well, I'll have to see." She picks up the phone on her desk and talks to somebody. "Just wait right over there," she tells us. "Mr. Grunman will be with you shortly." As we wait, she glances over at us several times, always looking quickly away as soon as we notice. I keep looking at the clock, worrying about Tim.

A young man comes out and talks to us, obviously not anybody very important. But after he looks at the picture, he takes us out of the reception area, through a heavy door into a corridor of offices. The actual TV studios must be back here somewhere.

We are taken into the office of somebody more important. This guy is middle-aged and harried, and the phone keeps ringing. But he looks at the picture. At first he goes pale, like everybody else. Then he gets excited. "Okay, start over again," he says, reaching for his computer keyboard. "Tell me the whole thing, from the beginning."

I talk, trying to tell the story concisely while not leaving anything important out. He types very fast. When I'm finished, he says, "Do you think you could loan us this drawing, let us show it on the air? It ought to attract people's attention. We'll run the photo of the missing boy again too."

This is exactly what I've been hoping for; I want as many people as possible to see Tim's drawing, because the heads said no one must see it. "Sure." Then another thought strikes me. "I just have to do one thing," I tell him. "Can I borrow a pen?"

He hands me a pen, and at the bottom of the drawing, where it won't hurt the artwork, I draw the letter *C* with a circle around it and write *Copyright Tim Coleman*. I do this so that we can sell the drawing. When I'm finished, I say, "I've got a more recent picture of Tim. I took it last night. This is what he looks like now. It might be interesting to show the one you already have and this one together."

He whistles when he sees the Polaroid of Tim. "You say this happened in two days?" he asks me.

"Uh-huh. Right, Mom?" I prod her with my foot again.

"Yes, that's right; I saw him before and after," she says firmly. "He . . . changed that much in two days."

The man stands up. "I've got to hurry if we're going to get this on the noon broadcast." He shakes our hands, then says to me, "You understand, we're just going to say this is what you believe. We can't say it's fact."

"Just be sure to mention the part about how I believe Tim's father is an alien, and show Tim's drawing and the photos too, if you have time. And be careful how you show the drawing. You know it only works when you look at it from the right angle."

"I'll see what I can do," the guy says, and we thank him and leave.

Dad is gone when we get home, and the phone has been fixed. Mom heads for the coffeepot. I'm too worried about Tim even to sit still. I'm also furious at the cops for not following Tim's father. That's obviously the way to find out where The Others are keeping Tim. I would have followed him myself if I'd had the chance.

But maybe after the newscast they won't hurt Tim.

Chapter Fifteen

It comes at the very end of the news, the least important spot, where they usually have some kind of humorous tidbit. The anchorman tries to make light of this story, but he can't really carry it off, since he too seems taken aback by the drawing. They keep it really short. They just say I claim Tim drew this picture on an alien ship, that he aged two years in two days, and that he was then taken away again by other aliens. They don't say I believe that his father is an alien, which is kind of too bad, but I didn't really expect they would—his father could probably sue them. They show the two photos of Tim, and then—most important—they show his drawing.

I'm nervous they'll botch it up somehow and that Tim's drawing won't come across. But, amazingly, they get it just right. Even though I've looked at it several times and know what to expect, it still shocks me when it appears on the screen. The sudden feeling of depth really comes across, the sensation of physically plunging down into the chasm. And all the awesome complexities of the ruined civilization, the heartbreaking details of the eroded and defoliated landscape, are clear and precise. The hideous creatures cavorting there are the final touch.

"Kind of makes you wonder if we might be next," the anchorman says when he's back on screen.

That remark never occurred to me, but I'm glad he said it. It might give people the idea the drawing means something.

I don't know whether or not the heads can intercept our broadcasts. If they can, they now know that thousands of human beings have seen Tim's drawing, against their orders. I wonder smugly how they feel about *that*.

The phone calls start soon after the news is over. I answer the first half dozen. After that I screen them with the answering machine, only picking up when the call is from a reputable newspaper or magazine. I keep the doors locked and don't agree to anything yet. I'm waiting for what I hope will be the next development.

I'm curious about how many phone calls Tim's father and mother are getting. Just for the heck of it, I dial their number. They have a new message: Tim's mother saying, "We are not who you are trying to reach. We are not returning any calls." If I didn't know what she was like, I'd think I was listening to an artificial voice synthesizer. I start to laugh when I hear it. Then I think about what might be happening to Tim, and the laughter catches in my throat.

But what I was hoping for happens sooner than I expected: That very evening, Tim's drawing makes the news on all three major networks, as well as cable. There are more phone calls than ever after that, and now they're from publications like *Time* and *Newsweek* and *Life*.

All day, when I'm not on the phone, I'm carefully writing the *C* with the circle around it and *Copyright Tim Coleman* on all of his drawings. I'm not planning to release any more of them for free.

Kroll also phones that night. He's furious about what I've done. "If your goal was to tie our hands so that we couldn't make a move in this search without attracting attention, you've succeeded," he tells me. "Don't you know this is exactly the kind of attention that kidnappers crave?"

"Alien kidnappers too?" I ask him.

He doesn't say anything.

"Come on, don't keep stalling," I say, hardly believing I'm talking to him this way—it's probably because I'm still angry he didn't follow Tim's father when he had the chance. "What did they find out about that implant?"

"Uh, very peculiar," he says after a long pause. "They can't identify any of the materials. It seems to be made of some kind of plastics nobody knows anything about. And the other thing . . ."

"Go on," I prod him.

"There's some kind of super micromechanism in it. Too small for anything in our lab to get a picture of. Nobody's ever seen anything like it. It's over at the university now, where they have an electron microscope."

I get the name of the lab at the university, so I can tell the reporters. "Now do you believe me about the aliens?" I can't resist asking Kroll.

"I'll talk to you later," he says and hangs up.

I made appointments with the reporters for tomorrow. Some local ones showed up today anyway, but I didn't let them in. When the doorbell rings at 11:30 P.M., we assume it's another reporter and ignore it.

Until Tim's father starts shouting to be let in again. I can hardly believe this is working out so perfectly.

I check to make sure there are no shapes outside the windows. Then I open the door an inch, without unfastening the chain, and peer outside. He seems to be alone. As soon as he comes in, I shut and lock the door behind him. "Where's Tim?" I ask him.

"Why are you asking me? I've got the whole police department out looking for him and—"

"I'm asking because you brought those creatures here last night to take him away."

"You're imagining things." Tim's father speaks slowly, which isn't like him. "Anyway, why are *you* cross-examining *me?* I came here to ask you why you stirred up all this media attention. Do you have any idea what you've done? I had to wait until now before I could get away from the house without being followed."

Mom and Dad are watching and listening, but they don't say anything.

Tim's father looks sick. He's extremely pale and haggard, with dark rings under his eyes. He even seems to have lost some weight, but it doesn't look good; the flesh of his face hangs from his bones. I wonder how much of this change in his appearance has to do with being hounded by reporters and how much might have to do with something else.

"I've just got to make sure you don't stir up any more trouble, Leo," he says, sounding a little out of breath. "If you have any more of those ridiculous drawings you erroneously claim were made by Tim, you'd better let me have them."

"So you can destroy them, right?"

"So I can make sure they don't get plastered all over the media and cause even more problems for us."

"Sorry. They're not here."

"Sure you're not lying, Leo? You're quite a skillful liar, I've learned."

Where did he get that idea? I never lie. . . .

Then it hits me. I just *did* lie, for the first time I can remember. How did it happen? It came out so naturally.

I try not to be shaken up by it. After all, this guy is the enemy. He's been lying all along, a lot worse than I am. "They're not here," I say again. I almost add, "And if they were, I wouldn't give them to *you*," but I'm not that stupid.

"If you have them here, I will use legal action to take them from you. After all, they were made by Tim. He's a minor. That means they are my legal property. I can have you arrested for—"

"I thought you said I *erroneously* claimed they were made by Tim."

"Well . . . uh, maybe I did. But—"

"I don't think you know what you're talking about. Go ahead and threaten me. I don't have them."

Tim's father's shoulders slump forward. He looks old.

"Of course, if you bring Tim back, then he might be able to stop them from broadcasting them or printing them in magazines or newspapers," I say. "But as long as he's gone, I'll make sure you can't turn on the TV or open a magazine without seeing them."

"How can I bring Tim back if I don't know where he is?" his father says, his voice dull. He turns and walks very slowly out the door.

"I want to follow him," I whisper the instant the door closes. "Can one of you come with me? We have to hurry. I've got to get something first." I start up the stairs.

"But why follow him back to his own house?" Dad asks me.

"Because that's not where he's going," I call back. Up in my room I quickly grab a couple of drawings out of the old backpack and put them in my current backpack. I run downstairs. Dad is waiting for me.

I don't turn on the headlights. Luckily, Tim's father is driving slowly; in the moonlight and the glow of a street-lamp, I can see his car at the end of the block when we pull out of the driveway. I keep about a block behind him. There are hardly any other cars out, and it's easy to keep him in sight.

Dad makes a noise of surprise when Tim's father does not turn onto their street. "You're right again, Leo," he says.

"He's leading us to Tim—and The Others," I say quietly.

We follow him out of town, past the industrial park and the black river that runs beside it. It's a good thing we have air-conditioning and the windows are closed; the smell is pretty bad around here.

Tim's father turns left into the trees, taking the narrow road along the riverbank. We have to be careful now; the road is deserted, and if Tim's father notices our car, he'll know he's being followed. I keep even farther behind him, following his lights in the darkness.

The lights of his car pull over to the left and blink out.

"Better if we walk from here," I say. I slow down to a crawl and park the car on the right shoulder of the road. I switch off the engine. We wait for a few minutes, hoping he will have gone inside whatever building might be there and won't hear the car doors close. Then we get out of the car and very quietly shut the doors.

We cross the road and walk about a hundred yards, to where Tim's father's car is. We don't say anything, though we both make gestures to each other of holding our noses and waving our hands in front of our faces. But I can guess why The Others would pick this place for their hideout: It stinks so much that most human beings keep away from here.

Tim's father has parked beside a derelict building that looks like it was once a small factory, built in the last century. It's made of brick, and the windows are boarded up. There is a big sign on it that says BUILDING CONDEMNED. NO TRESPASSING. The only light is a bare bulb in a little metal cage over a metal door.

"I guess it's stupid of me to hope it might be unlocked," I whisper. "If we can't get in, we'll just have to go back and get the cops."

"You can't go in there, Leo!" Dad says. "I won't allow it."

"I have to." I move toward the door.

I sense Dad hesitating, trying to decide what to do next. Then I hear his footsteps behind me. "I'm coming with you," he whispers. "There's no way I'm letting you go in there alone."

I reach the door. And that's when the momentum that's been pushing me ever since I cut out the implant begins to desert me. Suddenly I'm scared. And then I get an idea.

I turn back to Dad. "Why don't you go get the cops and bring them here. I mean, even if they don't believe us about the aliens, they'll be curious to find out what Tim's father is doing in this place. I'll wait here and see if I can get a look inside. I won't do anything risky."

Dad looks relieved. "Yeah, we could sure use the police." Then he frowns. "But you better come with me, Leo. I don't want to leave you here alone."

"It's better if I stay here—to be sure they don't get away or anything before the cops come."

"What would you do to stop them? You better come with me."

"I'm staying here, Dad. You don't understand. You haven't been with aliens, and I have."

He sighs. "Don't go inside, Leo," he says firmly.

"Don't do anything that would attract their attention. You promise?"

"Yeah, I promise," I say, feeling guilty about it. I'm lying again. And this time, it's not to the enemy; it's to my own father.

"I'll be back as soon as possible." He turns and sprints quietly away. Soon I hear the distant sound of the car starting. I'm assuming they can't hear it from inside the building.

I try the metal door. It opens.

Why isn't it locked? I can't believe Tim's father would just forget to lock the door, or that they would usually leave it unlocked. Either he is unbelievably careless—or he left it open on purpose, because he knew we were following him, and this is a trap.

But if I don't do anything until the cops come, it might be too late. The cops will probably make a lot of noise, and The Others will hear them and maybe transform themselves in some way and get away—probably taking Tim with them. I can't wait until the cops come and give our presence away. I have to catch The Others at whatever it is they're doing with Tim. And Tim's father was acting sick and confused, and he gave no indication he knew we were following him. He probably *did* just forget to lock the door. I try to convince myself that this isn't a trap.

Very, very slowly I begin to pull the door open. It makes a little noise, but only enough for somebody right inside to hear—and if they're right inside, I'm already out of luck. When it's open about a foot, I peer in. It's a long, dim corridor with doors on one side and one light on the ceiling, halfway down its length. The corridor is empty. I step quietly inside and start slowly down it.

I'm very tense. I keep looking back to make sure the way out is still unobstructed in case I suddenly have to run. I continue down the corridor, listening hard, hearing nothing to indicate there is anybody here at all.

"TAKE MY BLOOD," Tim's voice suddenly roars.

I jump about a foot into the air. It's all I can do not to scream.

The voice suddenly diminishes in volume. That's when I realize it's amplified. Somebody just turned on a recording of Tim's voice, with the volume too high. Now the volume is turned down, not loud enough for me to hear the words anymore, just the faint drone of it.

Then I see the light coming from the right side at the very end of the corridor. Maybe a door is open there. I move carefully toward it. Tim's voice grows louder.

As I get closer, it becomes more and more certain that the light is coming from an open doorway and that the recording is being played inside that room. "All the time. If not every day, then every other day," Tim's voice is saying.

I reach the doorway. Very carefully I peek inside with one eye.

Again, I barely keep from screaming.

Chapter Sixteen

TIM IS SITTING NOT FAR FROM THE DOORWAY on a folding metal chair in a large, sparsely furnished warehouse room, with wooden rafters and brick walls. He must be drugged or in a trance; his eyes are open, but he is staring straight ahead at nothing, and he is motionless. His father is slumped on another metal chair near him, his head in his hands. The tape recorder they are listening to is on a cheap folding table.

The nonhuman things in the room are crouching on the floor. There seem to be dozens and dozens of them. It's hard to tell how many, because the room is large and dimly lit.

I wonder if I am seeing The Others in their natural form. It's impossible to know, because Tim has told me they are shape changers, which I imagine means they can look any way they want. Still, it's hard to believe that any creatures would *want* to look like what I'm seeing now, if they weren't born that way.

They are the same as the creatures in the drawing that was on TV.

The things squat around Tim like toads as big as large

dogs, but with no skin on their bodies, so that the yellow muscle tissue and the purple veins are exposed; their webbed hands and feet are splayed on the floor. The toadlike, skinless aspect of their appearance in itself wouldn't be so bad—after all, I got used to the heads, who aren't exactly pretty—but the really disgusting, unspeakable part is the faces, the human faces, that stare directly up from the backs of their hunched-over bodies. The faces are about twice the size of human ones and horribly stretched out and deformed; the eyes stare blankly and pointlessly up at the ceiling. Are these their real faces or a part of their human disguise that they haven't sloughed off yet? I don't see any other things like alien faces on them; the creatures consist of four jointed limbs with webbed appendages and a back, upon which rests the human face. I recognize Dr. Viridian and also Herman, the man from the meeting at Annabelle Kincaid's.

Then something else hits me. Tim's father still looks completely human. Does that mean he just hasn't taken his disguise off? Or does it mean he really *isn't* one of them after all? If he isn't one of them, that would be even worse: It would mean he's a traitor to his own species and planet.

"Every time they brought me back from Sawan, they took my blood," Tim's voice is saying on the tape. "Every time they showed me something horrible and frightening, they took my blood. Every time they told me they were about to take me back to Sawan, to Chaweewan, they took my blood."

"And did they ever tell you why they took your blood

at these particular times, or what they were going to do with it?" a calm, restful voice asks him on the tape—the voice of the thing that calls itself Dr. Viridian.

"You asked me that before," says Tim's voice, with a hint of a whine, even though he is certainly in a trance.

"And I am asking you again."

"They never told me what they did with the blood. They only said it was because of The Others."

One of the creatures flops impatiently on the floor; another one makes a gurgling sound.

"You never eavesdropped on them?" asks the doctor's voice on the tape. "You never explored or spied on them? In the whole time you were with them, you never saw or heard anything you weren't supposed to? Think very carefully, Tim. Understand, you can remember absolutely everything now."

"No," Tim answers, after a moment. "I think I slept a lot on the ship. And when I was awake the bodies were always with me, watching me, taking my blood. And I was always very busy with my drawing."

The Dr. Viridian thing curses. "Those heads! If only they'd slipped up just once! They take human blood at moments of peak emotion—everyone they've abducted tells the same story. But why? Is it for a weapon? What are they doing?" It curses again, then stretches out one pair of legs, reaches up to the table, and switches off the tape recorder with its webbed fingers. I wonder how it can see what it's doing, since the human eyes on its back are not looking at the table but instead, now that its back is raised, toward the door. I quickly pull my head out of the doorway, praying it didn't see me. I stay just outside the door now, listening.

"And his precious drawings. What of them?" the Dr. Viridian thing says, hissing, and I hear its feet slapping on the floor. "So you had no luck tonight," it says, apparently addressing Tim's father.

"Leo claimed he didn't have any more of them," Tim's father says, sounding exhausted. "The lying little creep," he mutters.

"It will be disastrous if more people see those drawings. We will have to take the risk of getting them ourselves."

The voice is very frightening. Still, I feel a surge of excitement and pride. It seems like what I did was exactly the right thing; The Others as well as the heads don't want people to see the drawings. And tomorrow even more drawings will be released to the world; thousands more people will see them—assuming I ever get out of here.

"What could I do, search the house?" Tim's father is saying. "I used every threat I could think of. The stubborn brat wouldn't budge."

"And yet, even though you did not succeed in obtaining what we desperately require, you were still so careless that you allowed him to follow you here," the thing says.

"Follow me?" Tim's father says, sounding scared.

I'm scared too. I turn to run.

And am stopped by gray shapes rising up in the corridor, the same shapes that took Tim last night. I can't squeeze past them. They surround me; they pull at me. In the next instant I'm inside the room, the things squatting on the floor all around me. The gray shapes sink down; they bubble and writhe; they swell and change and become two more headless, toadlike things with human faces on their backs.

"Welcome, Leo," the Dr. Viridian thing says, its deformed face looking up at me, its mouth moving horribly. "You are getting sleepy. Your eyelids are getting heavy; soon you will be—"

I close my eyes and put my hands over my ears. "Stop it!" I shout. "You can't do this to me. You have to let Tim and me both go!"

"Not until we find out what we need to know." It says something in a wet language. One of the other ones moves toward me, and now I notice the syringe in its webbed fingers.

"No! Don't do that! I'll make a deal with you!"

"A deal?" the Dr. Viridian thing says suspiciously. "What kind of a deal, Leo?" But the one with the syringe doesn't come any closer.

"I have something you want, which I might let you see, if you don't try anything. Maybe I can get even more of them—if you let Tim and me go."

"I could kill you, Leo," Tim's father snarls at me.

"We'll take care of that," the Dr. Viridian thing says. "You're hardly in a position to bargain about anything, Leo," it goes on. "Tell us what you have before we take it from you."

I slip off my backpack, terrified. Now I don't know if I'm doing the right thing. The heads wanted me to give the drawings to The Others. The heads are their enemies. For that reason, I figured that letting The Others see the drawings would hurt them somehow. And now that I've made sure that thousands of humans have seen them, I figured it would be interesting to see what effect the drawings have on The Others.

I also stupidly thought I could use them as a bargaining tool. I was dead wrong about that. I have no power to bargain; I'm at their mercy—and it doesn't seem like they have much of that. As frightened as I was of the heads, they seem benign now compared to these things. They'll get the drawings I have in my pack, and they'll get me too.

I pull out a drawing. It's not one of the gruesome ones, unfortunately; it's a very realistic three-dimensional drawing of an alien farm. I figure Tim must have done it on Sawan, the rural, nontechnological planet where he was so happy. I hold it up under the light, so that all the many creatures squatting on the floor and lifting their hideous faces toward me in this large room will be able to see it.

For a moment there is absolute silence. Then suddenly they are all gurgling and hissing and howling and slapping their webbed feet on the floor. Their faces are twisted in disgust.

The Dr. Viridian thing, the closest to me, suddenly rears up and tears the drawing out of my hand and rips it to pieces. "We will get the others and destroy them!" it bellows. "We have searched all of Tim's memories. We know he left the rest of them at your house. But first we will deal with you."

They surge toward me, many of them brandishing syringes. I am screaming, backing up against the wall. There is no way to get away from them. Where are the cops? Why hasn't Dad come back with them yet? Now it's too late.

I am vaguely aware of Tim's father shouting, "Hey, hold on! Homicide might cause a little problem."

"He will drown naturally in the river!" roars the Dr. Viridian thing, its giant face rising up inches from me.

And then I feel the mist. It seems to be drifting down from the rafters. I feel the cool tingle of it on my face and arms; I feel it soaking into my shirt.

The Others can feel it too. They have stopped attacking me for the moment. They are looking around as if wondering where the mist could be coming from, shaking their limbs.

Suddenly the sensation hits everybody in the room at once: panic. It's like the feeling I had when I was abducted, the need to run, to scream, to get away, to be anywhere but where I am.

It's hardly any different from the way I felt just now, before the mist arrived. But clearly The Others are panicking too. They are flopping around in circles on the floor, moaning and bellowing. They seem to have forgotten about me completely. I want to run away, but there are too many of them between me and the door. Tim's father got away when he had the chance; he's bolting out of the room. Only Tim is still motionless, sitting in his chair.

One by one, the terrified Others begin to change. They writhe and bubble up and turn into the gray shapes—the gray shapes that look evanescent but still can't go through walls. The first ones get out the door easily enough. After that, there are so many of them that the door is blocked, and because they are panicking, they don't do anything but push and shove and try to get through. It's like a stampede of crazed animals. They are trapped for a long time in the bottleneck of the door, meaning I can't get out of the room, even though I am panicking too.

But somehow, I don't feel as panicky as The Others seem to be. I know I can't get out, so I don't try. I also don't want to desert Tim. In fact, maybe I can even wake him up. I go over and shake his shoulder. No response. "Tim," I say. "Hey, Tim. Maybe it's going to be okay. Something's scaring them away." I shake him. His head wobbles loosely. He does not come out of it.

I try something else. "On the count of three, you will be fully awake," I tell him. "One. Two. Three." Nothing happens. Now I am getting really worried about him. It is even stronger than the panic. If the Viridian thing hypnotized him, then maybe the Viridian thing is the only voice that can get him to come out of his trance. And now the Viridian thing is gone.

The bottleneck at the door has cleared up. The last gray shape flees from the room. I can get out now, but what am I going to do about Tim?

And then the cops come running in.

Chapter Seventeen

THE COPS DID ARRIVE IN TIME TO SEE THE LAST phantom shapes of The Others flying toward a purple sphere in the night sky—a sphere that quickly shrank away to nothing as soon as the last shapes reached it. The cops are stunned. They treat me differently now, of course, because now they believe my story. I'd feel smug, except that I'm so worried about Tim.

There were three carloads of cops, Dad tells me. They arrived just as Tim's father was driving away, and one cop car immediately took off after him. Kroll assures us it won't take them long to catch him.

I ride to the hospital in the cop car with Tim, the siren going full blast. Dad follows us and arrives a little later. In the emergency room they immediately hook Tim up to all kinds of equipment.

While we are waiting, Kroll phones Tim's mother. I can hear her hysterical voice over the phone. When she gets there, she is pale and disheveled and weeping. She is no longer the emotionless, perfectly groomed, zombielike creature she was on the night Tim disappeared; now she is behaving as I would expect a mother to behave. I wonder why she wasn't worried like this before, when Tim was missing. What has changed to make her behave this way?

She is also very confused. She doesn't seem to know anything about what has been happening.

Kroll keeps in close touch with the other cops. He leaves as soon as they report back to him that Tim's father has been brought to the station, ready to be questioned.

We wait at the hospital for hours, but there is nothing they can do to wake Tim up. His breathing and temperature and everything else are normal. He just won't wake up. In the morning, when Dad and I leave, they are saying he must be in a coma.

I'm so worried about Tim I don't even enjoy the press conference at our house that afternoon—the press conference that should be focused on Tim instead of me.

I tell the reporters and the TV interviewers everything I know about the heads and The Others. Kroll is there too. He won't say anything yet about Tim's father. But he publicly affirms that he saw the gray shapes last night. He also states that the implant from my ear represents a technology beyond anything known to the scientists at the university.

I don't know how much the reporters believe us. They think it's an interesting story, I guess, but they find it somewhat confusing. It's like they're disappointed

I'm not claiming the aliens came to destroy the Earth or to save the Earth. I don't know *what* either species of aliens came here for, and the media people don't like that. And they seem positively insulted when I tell them the heads said the Earth was completely irrelevant.

Kroll also says that Dr. Viridian and Dr. Pierce have vanished without a trace. There are no leads, nothing the cops can do to find them. The reporters consider this an odd coincidence. I'm hoping what it means is that The Others are really gone for good.

The magazines are clamoring for the rights to reproduce Tim's pictures on their covers. They are willing to pay a lot of money. Dad calls one of the top lawyers in town. Of course he knows about the drawings and is eager to represent Tim. He will have to draw up contracts, which will take several days at least. I am hoping that by that time Tim will be able to sign them. Since he is a minor, one of Tim's parents will have to sign them too. I don't doubt that they will be quite eager to sign, because of the large sums of money involved. I make sure the lawyer will put in the contracts that most of the money will be held in a trust fund for Tim, so that it will go directly to him when he reaches legal age.

Of all the people who are at our house today, I think the happiest are the representatives from environmental organizations. They keep beaming at me and saying that these drawings—the ones of ruined cities and landscapes, which have a deeply powerful effect on everybody who sees them—are one of the best things that has ever happened for the environmental movement. "If anything can save us, it might be those drawings," they keep telling me.

It almost makes me wonder if the heads were telling the truth when they said the earth was completely irrelevant to them.

One of the environmental guys, named Harrison, who has a ponytail, is particularly pushy. He keeps badgering Kroll about Tim's father. "That guy Coleman is *notorious*," Harrison says. "In the last few months, he's done more to hurt the environment than anybody else in this state."

Kroll just wants to get away from him, but I'm curious. "Exactly what has he done?" I ask Harrison.

"He's won cases for the factories that have put us back years, allowing them to dump toxic waste, things like that," Harrison tells me impatiently, as though I don't matter because I'm just a teenager. He turns quickly back to Kroll. "So what's the story on Coleman? What did he have to do with all this? Are you going to be able to stop him now?"

"I can't say anything about it at this time," Kroll says. "I have to go now." He turns abruptly and walks away.

"Exactly how much damage did Tim's father—" I start to ask Harrison. But he pays no attention to me; he hurries after Kroll.

It's late by the time everybody leaves, and Mom and Dad and I are exhausted. But I insist on going to the hospital. They argue with me, telling me there's nothing I can do to help Tim, but I won't give in, so Mom comes with me.

There are reporters there and cops to keep them out. The cops recognize us and let us through. Tim is in a private room now. We explain to the nurse on duty that we're Tim's friends, and since she knows the cops let us through, she doesn't ask any more questions. She tells us there has been no change in his condition and motions for us to go into his room.

Tim lies motionless on the bed, still hooked up to all kinds of gadgets. His mother is sitting on one side of the bed. His father is sitting beside her.

"Leo. Lenore," Tim's father says. "How good of you to come."

I can't believe what I'm hearing. My knees go so weak with surprise I have to steady myself against the wall; there is no available chair to sink into.

They are pale and disheveled now; they look almost dazed with grief and shock. I'm dying to know why they both seem so different and what happened to Tim's father at the police station. But first I say, "The nurse said there was no change."

Tim's father sighs. "No change," he says quietly. He takes his wife's hand and squeezes it. "I'd do anything to change what happened, to bring the lost time back."

"*What?*" The word explodes out of me.

"Leo. You're in a hospital," Mom says.

"Sorry," I say, remembering to keep my voice down. I'm more curious than ever now. "Uh, did you say *lost time?*" I ask Tim's father.

He nods, looking as though he might actually break down and cry. "Months and months. No memory. Both of us. The last thing we remember was the day I was asked to represent the Acme Chemical Company, and that was a good six months ago. The doorbell rang late that night; we thought it was odd, and I went to open it. I don't remember anything after that until last night, when I was driving by the river, and the police were chasing me. I pulled over right away. I had no idea what they were asking me at the station. Aliens? They put me on a lie detector. They got a doctor from this hospital who gave me some kind of truth drug and interviewed me under hypnosis. Nothing. But worst of all is what happened to Tim. I can't help feeling it's my fault somehow."

"Don't do that to yourself, dear," Tim's mother says, and they squeeze hands again. Then they both turn and gaze miserably at Tim.

"You don't remember *anything?*" I say.

"I think maybe we should go, Leo," Mom says.

She's right. We shouldn't bother them now. I'm not going to get anything out of him that the police couldn't. And we'll have to be seeing them again soon anyway.

Outside in the corridor Mom and I stare at each

other, both totally mystified. "What is going *on* with them?" Mom asks me.

"I wish I knew. Somehow they must have been under the control of The Others during the time they can't remember. Tim's father was working with them. But what was really going on? Why were The Others here? What was the point?"

We have to push through the reporters, ignoring their questions. They're still asking us things as we drive away. At home we go right to bed.

And I'm wondering, is this going to be it? I keep telling myself I might have to be resigned to the possibility of never finding out what was going on with The Others and what the heads were really doing here. At the same time, in my gut I have the pretty certain feeling I'll go nuts if I *don't* find out. In the last few days I've gotten accustomed to taking control of things, and I like the way it feels. It's horribly frustrating that there's nothing I can do to contact the heads and try to find out what their motives are and what The Others were trying to do. Thinking about it keeps me awake for hours.

And then I see the amber glow coming from some impossible place above the ceiling of my room.

CHAPTER EIGHTEEN

THIS TIME I DON'T PANIC. THIS TIME I'M NER-
vous but excited. I'm sure the heads will be even angrier
at me after what I've done, but I don't care. They know
they can't boss me around now, after I cut out their implant and did exactly the opposite of what they told me
to do . As I float up out of the roof of the house, I am
determined that I will find something out from them
this time, no matter what.

I enter the small craft waiting for me above the roof.
Tim is there! I'm so relieved to see him. He's still unconscious. But if anybody can wake him up, it is probably the heads.

The foliage on the mother ship is once again denser
and taller. It makes me wonder if the heads go away for
long periods of time in between the times we see them.
As usual, the bodies immediately take our blood and
strap us down onto the recliner.

"I know you're angry at me, but the most important
thing is to wake up Tim," I tell the heads right away,
before they even address me. "Nothing I did was his
fault; he's innocent. The Others did this to him. No

one in the hospital could wake him up. You've got to help him."

They still don't say anything to me. They must be *really* furious. One of the bodies undulates toward us with a device I haven't seen before. It looks sort of like a metal rattle, except that the rattle part is covered with dangerous-looking spikes. And now I *do* begin to panic. "Please don't hurt me!" I beg them. "I only did what I thought was right. And look what happened! The Others went away. Tim's parents are back to normal. And—"

At that point I see that the body with the dangerous-looking tool is aiming it at Tim, not me. It rolls the thing over Tim's head. It doesn't seem to cut him or hurt him. And a moment later Tim shakes his head. His eyes come into focus. He sees where he is. He sees me. His face is transformed by an expression of total joy; I've never seen him look anything like that before.

"I'm back! And you're here too, Leo!" he cries. "This is the best thing that ever happened!"

The bodies, meanwhile, are taking our blood again. Tim seems so used to it that he hardly notices. "Are you going to take me back there? To Sawan, to Chaweewan? Are you?" he is asking them.

They ignore his question. Instead, they address me. *Thank you, Leo. You have proven yourself to be a most resourceful person.*

"Huh?" I say. "You're not mad at me?"

Of course not. You did exactly the right things, much more ingeniously than we even expected.

"Yeah, but I did exactly the *opposite* of what you told me to do," I point out to them. "I mean, why didn't you just *tell* me what you wanted me to do, instead of telling me the opposite and hoping I'd go against it?"

We found from our tests of you that you are a very independent person and not one to take orders of any kind without reason—especially if the orders go against your own conscience. We also knew we had to keep secrets from you. If we told you our real plans and intentions, and you were then captured by The Others, they would find out too much. So we gave you orders we knew you would not want to follow, and we gave them in a manner we knew you would find unfair. You behaved as we had predicted—and more so.

And I thought I was being so forceful and taking control of things—when all the time the heads knew exactly what I was going to do. It's not only deflating; it's also a little scary that they could predict me so accurately. I don't like thinking about it.

And I'm curious about lots of other things. They are talking about keeping secrets from us—but now they are putting it in the past tense. "Maybe the need for secrets is over," I say. "Maybe you'll answer some questions now."

Ask, and we will see.

"What are The Others? What were they doing on the Earth? And are they gone now?"

The Others are beings that hunger for planets approaching environmental collapse. That is the atmosphere in which they thrive—as was evident in Tim's drawing. Sometimes they are instrumental in causing the collapse—that is what they did to our home planet. Sometimes they merely show up and bask in it and do what they can to help the process along.

I'm really getting excited now. Finally, some answers that make sense! Now I understand why The Others always hung out in places with the worst pollution—that's where they were most comfortable. I also understand why they gave all abductees such dumb, hard-to-believe memories; to protect themselves, they wanted as few people as possible to suspect that *any* aliens really exist. And now I know why they were controlling Tim's father to do everything he could to hurt the environment—and turning Tim's mother into a zombie so she wouldn't notice what had happened to his father.

It's also beginning to dawn on me that maybe the heads really are the good guys, after all.

In the case of the Earth, the human race needed little help from The Others to speed the destruction of the planet, the heads continue. *But of course The Others did what they could to help and to ensnare humans to help them, such as Tim's parents.*

"My parents?" Tim says.

"The Others were controlling them," I tell him. "That's why they were so weird. Didn't you notice any change in them, like about six months ago, when your father was asked to represent the Acme Chemical Company?"

Tim's eyes widen. "Six months ago? The middle of last winter?" He turns to me. "That's just about when they started acting so stiff and dressing up all the time and hardly ever sleeping. That's when they started hating my drawings! The Others were controlling them?"

I nod.

"And I was living in the same house with them," Tim says, sounding frightened. "Do you think, if The Others wanted them to, they could have killed me?"

I don't like thinking about it. "It's over now," I tell him. "But how do they do it?" I ask the heads. "How do The Others take people over like that?"

It's one of their secrets, like their shape changing. We don't know exactly how they do it, and that makes them very dangerous. What we do know is that they have to pick their slaves very carefully—they can't do it to very many people at the same time. But once they have picked someone, they can take that person over completely and almost instantly. And yes, Tim's parents would have killed him if The Others wanted them to.

"That's scary," I say, shivering.

It is, the heads agree. *But The Others have left your planet now. And now that they are gone, the drawings we taught Tim how to make will help to slow down the destruction of your planet, we think.*

"So you *did* come here to save the Earth, after all!" I
burst out.

Nothing of the kind! they say, as though the idea of-
fends them. *Our goal is to get back at The Others for what
they did to our planet and our species; to undermine all their
plans, to follow them everywhere and stop them from creating the kind of worlds in which they must live. That is our
assigned mission—and we do as we are told. We still find
the Earth completely irrelevant.*

"Was it you who created the mist that made The
Others run away?"

*Panic gas. We distilled it from your own blood and that
of others—blood taken from humans in moments of panic is
full of the most potent hormones. Turns out these hormones
have a devastating effect on The Others. We do not think
they will go back to the Earth now, for fear of experiencing
such pain there again. We do not have much in the way of
emotions ourselves, you see. We find emotions fascinating. So
we take samples of emotions whenever we can.*

"And now you're going to follow The Others some-
where else and stop them from wrecking another planet?
Not because you care about the environment, I know,"
I add quickly. "Just because you hate The Others."

*Exactly. We will follow them to Sawan. Of course the
Sawanese will be completely incompetent, the idiots. That
dull little planet will need all the help we can give them.*

"And you're taking us too?" Tim bursts out.

*Why should we take you? We have gotten what we
needed from you.*

"But you have to!" Tim shouts. "I have to see Chaweewan again. You can't do this! You take me there, you get me to love her—and then you won't take me back. It's not fair! It's inhuman!"

Who ever said we were human? If we have a reason to take you there again, we will. That is the end of it.

"But . . ." Tim protests. "But you . . . you . . . just can't . . ."

"Tim, listen to me," I tell him. "You don't know what happened while The Others had you. You're a world-famous artist now. I got your pictures on TV. You're going to be on the covers of all the big magazines. You'll be rich. And you're better than rich—your pictures are what might save the Earth."

"Huh?" Tim says. "Is that really the truth?"

It is the truth, the heads affirm.

"Tim, you have contracts to sign. It's going to be the most exciting time in your life. You don't want to miss it. And they said they *might* take you back someday."

That is what we said. And now we must go. Thank you both for all your help.

The cables unwrap. We rise into the air. We float to the smaller ship.

"I can't believe they're doing this," Tim moans as we descend.

"Oh, stop it!" I say, irritated with him again. "We're both going to be heroes. It's the best thing that ever happened to us. Not to mention, your parents are back to normal again, now that The Others are gone. Just relax and enjoy what's happening and stop wishing you were somewhere else. Not that you have much choice."

"Well . . . we'll see," he says petulantly.

But I'm too happy to stay irritated with him. Even if he won't admit it, I know that we are about to enter the most exciting time in our lives. And now that we're safe from The Others and all my questions are answered, I'll really be able to enjoy every minute of it.

It's just beginning to get light when I land back in bed. I'm too excited to try to sleep, and anyway, I'm starving—I can't remember the last time I had a real meal.

I hear noises from the kitchen as I go downstairs. That's odd. Mom and Dad never get up this early, and they both went to bed very late last night.

Mom is in the kitchen. She is heavily made up; her hair is perfectly groomed; she is wearing a freshly ironed dress and stockings and high heels.

"Good morning, Leo," Mom says in a flat, expressionless voice. "What would you like for breakfast today."

William Sleator says, "This book was very easy for me to write because They told me exactly what to say. I just wrote it down the way They wanted it. And They told me if it got published, They would come back and take me away again. So now I'm waiting. They promised They would come. They *have* to come!"

While Mr. Sleator bides his time, he lives in Boston, Massachusetts, and Bangkok, Thailand.